P9-DET-659

Growing up, Monica had been resolutely off-limits...

Monica tipped her head and all that gloriously long and stick-straight blond hair slid over her shoulder. "I'm sorry I didn't make it to Cole's funeral."

"It's not like we live close anymore. Five hours' drive round-trip makes for a long day."

Cash glanced at Monica and caught the turmoil in her face. "You okay?"

She nodded. "What can I do?"

He narrowed his gaze. "Not much you can do. These things happen."

"I meant dinner. How can I help?"

He blew out his breath, glad for a reason to escape the trip down a pain-filled memory lane. "You can help by making patties, and I'll get the grill going."

"Deal."

Out on the deck, the sun hung low in the sky. Leaning against the railing, Cash wondered why Monica would come up here by herself. Part of him hoped she would stay.

The other part worried that being around Monica for very long was asking for trouble.

Jenna Mindel lives in northwest Michigan with her husband and their three dogs. A 2006 Romance Writers of America RITA® Award finalist, Jenna has answered her heart's call to write inspirational romances set near the Great Lakes.

Books by Jenna Mindel

Love Inspired

Maple Springs

Falling for the Mom-to-Be
A Soldier's Valentine
A Temporary Courtship
An Unexpected Family
Holiday Baby
A Soldier's Prayer

Big Sky Centennial

His Montana Homecoming

Mending Fences
Season of Dreams
Courting Hope
Season of Redemption
The Deputy's New Family

Visit the Author Profile page at Harlequin.com.

A Soldier's Prayer

Jenna Mindel

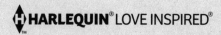
HARLEQUIN® LOVE INSPIRED®

If you purchased this book without a cover you should be aware that this book is stolen property. It was reported as "unsold and destroyed" to the publisher, and neither the author nor the publisher has received any payment for this "stripped book."

Recycling programs for this product may not exist in your area.

LOVE INSPIRED BOOKS

ISBN-13: 978-1-335-47936-5

A Soldier's Prayer

Copyright © 2019 by Jenna Mindel

All rights reserved. Except for use in any review, the reproduction or utilization of this work in whole or in part in any form by any electronic, mechanical or other means, now known or hereafter invented, including xerography, photocopying and recording, or in any information storage or retrieval system, is forbidden without the written permission of the editorial office, Love Inspired Books, 195 Broadway, New York, NY 10007 U.S.A.

This is a work of fiction. Names, characters, places and incidents are either the product of the author's imagination or are used fictitiously, and any resemblance to actual persons, living or dead, business establishments, events or locales is entirely coincidental.

This edition published by arrangement with Love Inspired Books.

® and TM are trademarks of Love Inspired Books, used under license. Trademarks indicated with ® are registered in the United States Patent and Trademark Office, the Canadian Intellectual Property Office and in other countries.

www.Harlequin.com

Printed in U.S.A.

Nay, in all these things we are more than conquerors through him that loved us.
—*Romans* 8:37

For those who have run or are running the race.

Acknowledgments

My special thanks to Chrystianna
for telling great stories of her two boys.
They were my inspiration for Ethan and Owen.

Huge thanks to Aunt Colleen
for her insight and knowledge of the process
surrounding a diagnosis for breast cancer.
I really appreciate it. Love you!

Chapter One

Monica Zelinsky had to get away and think. *Think*. She had just turned thirty and yet life as she knew it was over. From here on out she'd be considered a cancer survivor. If she survived. If the cancer didn't spread. She prayed it wouldn't.

Running a hand through her long hair, she grabbed a handful and pulled hard enough to sting. She'd lose this. She'd lose it all, after she'd spent over a hundred and fifty dollars for a highlight. Sure, it might be crazy to think of measly dollars when she faced a much bigger cost, but she couldn't help it. Getting her hair done had always been something she'd looked forward to.

Keeping her gaze fixed on the road ahead watching for the turnoff, she gave full vent to her fears with a disgusted growl. Hair grew back. Her breasts wouldn't, and removing them was one of the options she had to consider. She'd need chemo regardless of her surgery choices, having been diagnosed with an aggressive form of breast cancer.

This kind of news should alter a person's priorities real quick, but it didn't do a thing to dissolve Monica's insecurities. She'd never been comfortable with her looks, and now… She blew out another breath. She'd get even more uncomfortable before it was all over.

Tightening her grip on the steering wheel until her knuckles turned white, Monica took the two-track road that led to her uncle's cabin in the middle of the Upper Peninsula of Michigan.

She had a little less than a week before meeting with a referred cancer team to go over her *plan of attack*, they'd called it. A war waged inside her body called triple negative breast cancer. She was considered stage two out of four, and so far no lymph nodes were affected. She'd had no idea, no symptoms—not even family history—to give her a heads-up. This had come out of the blue with nothing to tip her off to a problem until she'd found the hard lump in her right breast.

Monica barely noticed the changing color on the trees. It was late August, but fall came early in the UP. Just like this cancer had come way too early in her life.

Cutting the engine, she got out and stretched.

It had been a three hour drive north and west into the middle of nowhere. Her uncle's cabin sat deep in the Hiawatha National Forest that ran between Munising and Escanaba. She knew the way by heart. She'd been coming here since she was a kid with her family, mostly her older brothers, especially Matthew. He was the keeper of the cabin keys for her family, although for this visit, Monica had to get a set directly from her uncle.

Scanning the chalet-style log cabin with its dark green metal roof, Monica looked forward to a few days of solitude and more online research. She would pray, think and pray some more, and hopefully prepare for what lay ahead. She was definitely short on courage these days, especially after Brady dumped her.

After being interested in him for years, Monica was happy when Brady had finally asked her out, and things had been pretty good. At least she'd thought so. They'd been dating for months now, but he couldn't handle her cancer sentence and had cut her loose. His departure should hurt, but Monica was more disappointed than anything. She'd hoped for love but that hadn't happened. Brady hadn't been right for her. Too bad. She would have appreciated a broad shoulder to lean on.

Stepping inside the cabin, she noticed the window over the sink in the kitchen had been left open. A sink that was full of dirty dishes. Her brothers had been here earlier this summer, but surely they hadn't left the place like this.

She climbed the knotty pine staircase leading to a cozy loft and dumped her suitcase on one of four beds. Staring out the floor-to-ceiling windows, she smiled. She'd always loved the loft because she could see the vast out-of-doors even at night, catching a glimpse of the stars.

She trudged back to her car for the groceries she'd brought, including a small cooler. Before putting the items away she texted her mother that she'd made it safely. There were several cell service dead zones in the area, but fortunately, her uncle's cabin wasn't one of them. She then checked her office messages that were forwarded to her cell. She ran her own web design and branding business, but there was nothing that couldn't wait until Monday.

Opening the fridge door to transfer the cooler contents, she noticed that it was already stocked. The gallon of milk on the top shelf was nowhere near out-of-date. In fact it looked like a recent purchase. Odd. Monica's sister-in-law said that Matthew had the keys with him. At least that's what Annie had thought when Monica stopped by their house to pick them up. She quickly texted her brother to ask if anyone else had come up here. He worked as a first mate on a Great Lakes freighter, so she didn't expect an answer right away.

Stepping down the short hallway, she checked the other two bedrooms. The larger one looked neat and tidy, with the bed made, the coverlet wrinkle-free, and shoes lined up under a bench that held a duffel bag. The other room was a mess—bunk beds unmade, suitcases open and kids' clothes strewn about. No one in her immediate family had small children. Babies and toddlers, yes, but not kids big enough for those clothes.

Who on earth was here, and why?

Cash Miller looked at his two little nephews buckled into booster seats in the back of his Dodge Challenger. Ethan was eight and Owen had just turned five. Cash was giving his sister-in-law a break for a long weekend before she and his mother joined them at the cabin for the rest of the following week. Cash hoped that a *men's* camping trip might loosen Owen's now silent tongue.

Owen had a chocolate ice cream stain all over the front of him. The kid had taken forever to eat his cone and couldn't keep up with the drips.

"Mom's going to be mad when she sees your shirt," Ethan taunted.

"No, she won't," Cash said.

"Everyone knows you're just acting stupid." Ethan kept badgering his little brother.

"Don't call your brother stupid." Cash looked at the eight-year-old through the rearview mirror.

Ethan glared back. "He can talk."

Cash held back from correcting him. Owen used to talk a blue streak, right up until his father, Cash's only sibling, had died a few weeks ago. The mind could play nasty tricks and Cash figured the stress Owen suffered from had manifested into a physical thing, affecting his speech. One he hoped wouldn't remain permanent. It had to be a phase.

He gritted his teeth and silently prayed. *God, please let this be a short-lived phase. Help me this weekend. I could really use some help.*

One more glance at Owen's T-shirt and Cash was pretty sure he could get the stain out. Even if he couldn't, his sister-in-law wouldn't be mad. Ruth had been beyond relieved when he volunteered to take the boys off her hands for a few days so she could settle his late brother's estate without distractions. Though his mom lived with Ruth, she wasn't handling Owen's silence very well, so Cash had stepped up to help. He had to.

"Uncle Cash?" Ethan's pot-stirring voice twisted his gut.

What was he up to now? "Yeah, dude?"

"Do you think Dogman will find us at the cabin?"

Cash glanced at Owen. The little guy's dark eyes widened with fear. He could have cuffed Ethan upside the head for spooking Owen with that old Michigan legend. "No. He won't find us because Dogman isn't real."

"Yes, he is, Uncle Cash. My dad said so," Ethan challenged.

Cash clenched his jaw to keep from saying something he shouldn't. His older brother, Cole, had loved telling stories. He used to scare Cash as a kid, much like Ethan did to Owen. "What your dad said was make-believe. Just pretend."

Ethan scowled and didn't say another word.

Cash swallowed his own rising anger. He'd had his fill of death and dying. A marine since he'd graduated from high school, he'd seen his share of friends go down, including his first commanding officer, who'd been like a father figure to him. It made getting too close to people a really dumb idea. There one moment, gone the next.

Losing Cole, who'd been in the prime of his life, to a freak logging accident wasn't something Cash had expected, much less prepared for, and it hurt. It hurt real bad.

He'd taken leave for his brother's funeral, but now faced the task of helping his nephews accept that their dad was gone for good. Ethan acted out, while Owen had retreated. Regressed, Ruth had called it. Cash had some experience with brothers in arms who'd reacted similarly, but he was no expert. All he knew was that grief had a way of leaking out in strange forms.

Like now. Hearing that Dogman legend tore him up pretty good. The fictional spooky creature was said to linger in the woods of the Lower Peninsula, but folks liked to spread tales of sightings in the Upper, as well. Cole was probably one of them spreading those rumors, considering he'd spent a lot of time in the woods. Owning a forestry business, Cole had been an expert woodsman. He shouldn't have died like he did, toppling a tree that had twisted backward and fallen on him.

Cash gritted his teeth once again until he got control. He had a job to do and that was keeping two little boys busy with fun for the next four days.

As Cash pulled into the driveway, he spotted a sporty blue Subaru and his thoughts skidded to a halt. They had company.

"Who's here?" Ethan was out of the car in seconds, running toward the door.

Owen moved much slower, looking wary.

Cash scooped up the five-year-old and followed Ethan inside the cabin. He nearly ran the kid over, because Ethan had stopped cold and was staring ahead.

"Is she a princess?" he whispered.

Owen inhaled sharply.

Cash also stared at the ethereal vision before them, of sunlight pouring in a window behind a tall female with long blond hair. Her slender outline glowed golden in the late afternoon light and the sequined T-shirt she wore shimmered like diamonds.

She made quite the royal vision in jeans and that T-shirt, but one he recognized well. "No, boys. That's no princess, it's Monica Zelinsky. How are you, Stork?"

"Nice." She sneered at the old nickname he'd given her when they were kids. "Cash Miller, is that really you under all that facial hair?"

"In the flesh." He hadn't shaved since he'd left base and had a bit of a beard going. He tried to let Owen down, but the kid clung to him.

"It's been ages." Monica stepped forward, out of the haze of golden sunlight. "Who do you have there?"

He'd always thought her attractive, even when she'd been a long-legged, skinny teen. The last time he'd seen her was over two years ago, at her brother's wedding. Monica had been overly made up and stuffed into a shiny dress. Taking in the sequins on her T-shirt, he figured she liked the sparkle. She didn't need all the glam. She shone from within and always had.

He cleared his throat. "My nephews. The older one is Ethan, and this little dude is Owen."

"Hello." Monica smiled.

Cash's pulse kicked into high gear. That smile of hers always had the power to knock him off-kilter.

She scrunched her nose. "I'm sorry. I didn't know anyone would be here. Should I leave?"

"*No.*" Hadn't he just prayed for help? It was as if God had answered that prayer by bringing her here. Bringing help until the boys' mom and grandmother arrived. No way could she go. "Stay. Please. We're going to grill out for dinner."

Monica's bright blue eyes narrowed. She looked torn, as if staying or leaving played a tug-of-war inside her head.

Cash wouldn't blame her if she left, but he didn't want her to. Not only could he use her help, but it'd been a long time since he'd seen her. He wouldn't mind catching up a little.

She crouched down so she was eye level with Ethan. "What do you think? Do you mind if I stay for dinner?"

Ethan still gazed at her as if he expected a crown to materialize on her head. "I don't mind."

Monica stood and faced Owen, smiling once again. Her teeth were perfect and bleached white. She'd been one of two Zelinsky kids who had needed braces. "And what about you? Owen, is it?"

Owen hid his head against Cash's neck, but he nodded.

"He's sort of quiet these days." Cash gave her a look that said he'd tell her later.

"Owen won't talk. He hasn't since our dad died," Ethan answered.

"Oh. I'm so sorry." Monica looked sad. Really sad.

Her bright eyes had always been expressive. Her smart mouth, too. He remembered that there wasn't much Monica wouldn't say, and that's what had endeared her to him when they'd first met. He'd been fourteen and she'd been ten.

Cash set the boy down and spread his arms. "There you have it, the Miller dilemma. Why don't you guys go wash up and then we can get the burgers made for the grill. Ethan, see that Owen changes his shirt."

The boys ran for their room, feet stomping and door banging.

Monica smirked as she poked a spot of melted ice cream in the middle of Cash's T-shirt. "I see you had ice cream before dinner."

He tensed under her touch. "That's what uncles are for."

She cupped his shoulder and gave it a squeeze. "I'm so sorry about Cole."

"Thanks." Tempted to draw her to him, he stepped back instead.

Other than a shared embrace when she'd turned eighteen, Cash hadn't hugged Monica since his father died when he was sixteen. Not only was she four years younger than him, making such things a little awkward, but any guy worth his salt didn't mess with his best friend's little sister. *Not ever.* Growing up, she had been resolutely off-limits.

Fast forward several years and his change of career from an enlisted marine to the Marine Corps Forces Special Ops Command made serious relationships with women off-limits, as well. At least for him. Becoming a Marine Raider had been his choice, just like steering clear of Monica ever since that one kiss they'd shared on her eighteenth birthday...

"Cash?"

"Huh?" Had she been talking?

"I'm sorry I didn't make it to Cole's funeral." Monica tipped her head and all that gloriously long and stick-straight blond hair slid over her shoulder.

She had always been taboo, and it sure felt like she should be now. He experienced that familiar nip of awareness and like always, he brushed it aside, refusing to let the attraction grow.

"It's not like we live close anymore. A five-hour drive round-trip makes for a long day." Although Cash had been glad to see her parents there at the church. Matthew had made it because he was catching his freighter at port in Marquette the following day.

Ethan and Owen came tearing into the kitchen.

"Give it back!" Ethan chased his little brother who scooted out of reach waving a fidget spinner.

"Guys, tone it down." Cash ran his hand over his whiskered chin. He'd shave when he had to, when he returned to duty on Labor Day, in a little over a week.

The boys tore into the living room.

Owen threw the fidget spinner at Ethan. Then the boys launched themselves onto the couch and clicked on the TV. The fight was over as quickly as it began.

He glanced at Monica and caught the turmoil in her face. "You okay?"

She nodded. "What can I do?"

He narrowed his gaze. "Not much you can do. These things happen."

Again, the teasing smirk. "I meant dinner. How can I help?"

He blew out his breath, glad for a reason to click off the trip down his pain-filled memory lane. "You can help by making patties while I get the grill going."

"Deal." Monica looked into the living room. "Ethan and Owen, do you want to help?"

Ethan groaned, but Owen slipped off the couch and tiptoed toward Monica.

Cash exited the cabin onto the deck. The sun hung low in the sky, but it wouldn't set for another couple hours. He turned on the gas valve, then lit the grill and shut the lid.

Leaning against the railing of the deck, Cash wondered why Monica would come up here by herself. He'd have to ask her later, if she stayed beyond dinner. Part of him hoped she would. The other part worried that being around Monica for very long was asking for trouble.

"Thank you, Owen." Monica's heart melted when the boy smiled, then walked the plate of hamburgers outside for Cash to place on the hot grill.

He might not speak, but the little boy was a charmer, with rich red hair and thick eyelashes that framed dark gray eyes. Eyes a lot like his uncle's.

Through the sliding glass door to the deck out back, Monica watched Cash cup his nephew's cheek as he took the plate from him. Despite his rough-and-tumble ways, Cash was a gentle guy. Even though he'd been Matthew's friend, he'd always taken time to talk with her. He'd made her feel awkward, sure, especially the year she grew to be taller than him by a couple inches or so, but he never made her feel unwanted. Never the annoying tagalong that she'd often been.

The last time she'd seen Cash Miller was two and a half years ago, at her brother Matthew's wedding. There hadn't been any dancing and Cash had pretty much ignored her after a brief greeting. He'd hung out with her brothers and then left before she'd had a chance to really talk to him. She wouldn't mind spending a little time with him now, just to make sure he was okay, and hear what he'd been up to.

"How do you know Uncle Cash?" Ethan climbed onto the stool on the other side of the island.

"Your uncle is friends with my brother. I've known him since I was a little older than you."

Ethan gave her a haughty glare from golden-colored eyes. He, too, had a mop of red hair, although lighter than his little brother's. "I'm eight."

"I was ten when I first met your uncle Cash." Monica grabbed the bag of spring mix she'd purchased, along with some veggies.

She would never forget the day Matthew had brought Cash home with him from school for the first time. Cash had taken one long look at her and called her a stork. She'd been furious at that moniker because it had been far too accurate. She had been a skinny kid with even skinnier legs, crooked teeth and a big nose. She still had the big nose.

"There's frozen french fries in the freezer." Cash entered the kitchen, opened the fridge and grabbed a can of pop, snapping open the tab top with a fizzy click.

"Yeah, so?" Monica tipped her head.

"So, I thought you could make them." Cash winked at Ethan.

The boy looked at her, then back at Cash with a grin.

"Why can't *you* make them?" Monica wasn't giving in that easily. Especially in front of an eight-year-old watching them with too-wise eyes.

"I'm manning the grill."

"You're in here now, with plenty of time to take care of the fries while I set the table."

"The boys and I eat in the living room." Cash completely evaded her comment.

"Yeah," Ethan added, with challenge in his voice.

Monica glanced at Owen, now lying on the couch watching a cartoon on TV, then back at Cash. "What would their mother say?"

Cash rolled his eyes.

Monica had her answer. She wasn't the boss of any of them, so she merely took plates and set them on the island, while Cash grabbed the bag of frozen fries.

Ha! She'd won that round.

The space between the stove and island was limited. Her breath caught when she turned to fetch the silverware and collided with Cash leaning to throw the empty fries bag in the trash can under the sink.

Cash straightened and gestured for her to go first. "After you."

Despite her hot cheeks and Ethan's giggle, she managed a sarcastic-sounding retort, "Why don't you get out of the kitchen?"

He winked at her. "Exactly what I was hoping you'd say."

Monica tried to ignore him. She tried even harder to ignore the pesky increase in her heart rate, but that was a lost cause and had been ever since she was twelve.

She opened the fridge to gather condiments, then

whipped around to set the bottles on the island. Cash was in her space once again. She dodged left, but he lurched the same way. Bobbing the opposite direction, they did an awkward dance that ended with her dropping the ketchup bottle.

Cash bent to retrieve it at the same time she did and they bumped heads.

"Oww!"

He laughed and gently touched her forehead with his fingers, rubbing where they'd hit. "I'm so sorry."

She looked into his dark gray eyes filled with mirth and the truth slipped out. "You're dangerous, Cash Miller. That's what you are."

His gaze darkened as it swept her face.

And there it was—that sting of awareness she knew well. Monica could barely breathe as she recalled the one kiss they'd ever shared. It had been her eighteenth birthday party and her parents had hosted a huge cookout. She'd walked Cash to his car because he'd had to head back to base. There, he'd given her the most beautiful crystal stork. To thank him for such a lovely gift, she had hugged him, and that embrace had soon turned into the most wonder-filled kiss she'd ever received.

Did he remember it, too?

She shut down that train of thought quickly. She couldn't go there. Not now, not ever. She had a nasty medical battle ahead. One that had already chased away one guy she thought she could rely on. There was no way she'd let another man, especially *this* man, mess her up when she was plenty worried about her future as it was. If she even had a future long enough to enjoy.

Tamping down the panic that crept upon her ever since she received the bad news of her biopsy, Monica set the bottles on the island. Ketchup, mustard, squeez-able mayonnaise, ranch and Thousand Island salad dressing all toppled over.

Ethan reached out to help her right them.

That's when Monica saw the smoke. Glad for the di-version, she hid behind her trusty sarcasm. "Uh, Cash? You better check those burgers."

He dashed for the deck and opened the barbecue lid. Flames shot up as he flipped the burgers over.

Monica looked at Ethan. "I hope you like yours well done."

Ethan shrugged.

Monica got busy grabbing cups and the gallon of milk. Anything to keep her focus away from Cash. No way could she stay here the whole weekend. She'd never functioned well around him and it looked as if that still held true.

She'd stay tonight and tomorrow morning tops, then she'd be on her way. Maybe she'd head for a motel in Marquette. It was a pretty college town on the shore of Lake Superior. But Monica didn't need pretty. She needed to think things through, do more research and jot down a million more questions. She needed to find some kind of inner strength to deal with what lay ahead. Other than her family's support, she faced this disease alone. Could she beat it? Monica wasn't sure.

All she knew was cancer waged a war inside her and she was scared. Really scared.

Chapter Two

Monica felt a soft touch and looked down into the pleading eyes of Owen. "What is it?"

He pulled on her hand.

"He wants to show you something," Ethan offered.

No kidding. Monica bit her tongue and played along, following the little boy.

Owen led her to the TV, which had gone blank even though the satellite box dials glowed blue, showing it was still active. The TV was old and the picture sometimes grayed out, needing to be reset. It usually came back on after someone turned the whole thing off for bit, but maybe this time it had burned out for good.

"You know what, how about we turn off the TV for now? I imagine you didn't come here with your uncle Cash to watch TV." Monica looked down at the boy. Why were they here? She'd never known Cash to hang around little kids before.

"The burgers are done and not too burned." Cash entered with the plate.

"The TV's out, so we might as well eat at the table," Monica said. "Owen, would you like to help me?"

The boy nodded.

"He sure likes you." Cash leaned close and whispered teasingly, "He probably thinks you really are a princess. Storks can look regal, you know."

Monica laughed when she considered her just-over-six-foot frame. "There's more giant than princess about me."

"A more beautiful giant there never was, right, Owen?" Cash grinned when his nephew agreed with wide eyes.

Monica soaked in the compliment, but shook her head at Cash's nonsense. He'd have the poor boy wondering if she really were a giant. If she remembered correctly, giants were to be feared in storybooks. In a few months, she'd look pretty scary from chemo.

With a sigh, she handed Owen a glass of milk, with directions to place it on the table. She did the same with Ethan, who complied, but that's as far as his help went. He slid into a chair at the table as if he expected to be waited on.

Monica ignored that idea and helped Owen fix his plate as Cash pulled the cookie sheet of french fries from the oven. They were burned a little on the ends, but to her they looked perfect.

Cash started to make a plate for Ethan, but Monica stalled him. "Ethan, if you'd like dinner you're going to have to come get it."

Cash stared at her as if she'd called the kid a bad name.

"Really, there's no need to wait on them. We fixed the food. They can come get it." Monica was the sixth of ten kids. Growing up with three younger brothers and one younger sister, she'd learned early on to follow her mother's example. Helen Zelinsky did not believe in babying anyone.

Ethan looked at Cash for support.

Thankfully, he backed her up. "You heard her."

Ethan glared at Monica, but stayed put, arms folded.

"Now you've done it," Cash muttered under his breath.

So much for Cash's alliance, but Monica wasn't about to give in. "Does their mom wait on them?"

Cash nodded. "Hand and foot."

"No wonder she needed a break," Monica muttered as she dished salad onto her plate, then offered a spoonful to Owen.

Once both their plates were filled, she handed Owen his and followed his slow steps to the table. The tyke didn't drop a single fry, so praise was definitely in order. "Good job."

He beamed at her.

Monica waited for Cash to sit down. Ethan's scowl deepened. "Can we say *grace*?"

Cash bowed his head. "You do it."

Owen folded his hands.

Ethan looked at the ceiling.

Monica bowed her head and recited the dinnertime prayer she'd known her whole life. "Bless us, O Lord, and these Thy gifts, which we are about to receive from Thy bounty, through Christ our Lord. Amen."

"Amen." Cash made a show of digging into his food noisily. "This is really good, Ethan. You better get yours."

"I'm not hungry." He slumped a little lower.

"That's a shame." Monica bit into her hamburger.

After a few minutes, Ethan sighed and finally dragged himself to the island, where his plate holding a hamburger waited to be filled with fries and salad. He grabbed a handful of salad and plopped it on his plate, then squirted ranch dressing all over it before grabbing a handful of fries.

When he slipped back into his chair, Monica gave him a beaming smile. "Thank you."

Ethan didn't say anything, but she thought a whisper of a smile tugged at his mouth.

She caught Cash's gaze from across the table and he tipped his head to her. Another round won.

This certainly wasn't the weekend she'd envisioned, but a cold motel room didn't sound any better and she really didn't want to head back home. Not yet, anyway.

After dinner, they all pitched in to clear the table. Even Ethan helped put stuff away without complaint, while she filled the sink with hot soapy water and Cash banged on the TV until it finally turned on again.

The boys rushed to throw themselves on the couch, pushing each other, giggling.

Cash brought her an empty glass left on one of the end tables. "You're really good with the boys. You'll make a good mom one day."

"Thanks." Monica's voice nearly betrayed her, so she focused on her newly manicured nails, painted deep orange, while she got control of her emotions.

She might not ever have kids of her own, if the chemo fried her insides. Then again, she might never marry if she went under the knife to be butchered. What man would find her body acceptable after that?

"I'm glad you're here." Cash patted her back. It was a friendly sort of gesture, but awkward.

Monica wanted to know if he meant it. "Are you really?"

His gaze narrowed. "You showing up like you did was an answer to a prayer."

"Yeah?" She wanted to tell him to keep praying, because she needed it, but the words stuck in her throat.

"Yeah." Cash nodded.

She didn't want him to know what she faced, because if she started to unload, she might cry. Monica never cried if she could help it, and Cash would definitely freak out if she did. She smiled at the thought of knocking Cash's tough-guy exterior askew. It might be worth it just to see what happened, but she didn't want his worry or his pity.

Monica had to accept that this cancer was her burden to bear. Alone.

Cash stared at the stack of dishes next to the sink and then glanced at the boys on the couch. "Ethan, Owen, we're not done yet."

"Do we have to?" Ethan dropped his head back and groaned.

Owen skipped forward, eager to help.

The little guy rarely disobeyed, and Cash wondered if that was why he seemed to have lost his ability to speak. Was silence his way of showing defiance, or an attempt to regain some kind of control over his young life?

"If you want to roast marshmallows, we have to clean up our lunch and dinner dishes." He glanced at Monica and smiled.

She smiled back as she stepped toward the sink. "If we all pitch in, it will go faster."

"Exactly." Cash took one look at her perfectly painted fingernails and nudged her out of the way. "I'll wash. You three can dry and put away."

Monica saluted him. "Aye, aye, sir."

"That's 'First Sergeant, sir.'" He squirted more soap into the already hot and soapy dishpan and swished his hand to make more bubbles.

"Wow, you're marching right up the ranks, huh?"

Cash shrugged. He'd been at this rank for a while now, leading his team.

"When do you go back?" Monica handed out clean dish towels to the boys for drying.

"I've got another full week of leave. I have to report on Labor Day."

Her eyes clouded over. "Not long then."

"I took a month, considering the circumstances." Cash dumped the silverware into the tub with a clatter.

"How many years has it been for you?"

"Since I enlisted?" He grabbed the cups next, scrubbing each one and placing it in the second sink.

Monica nodded.

"Fifteen years." He had five more to go before he could even think about retiring, not that he would.

He didn't know what he'd do if he ever retired. He was a soldier, a *Raider* of the Marine Corps Forces Special Ops. A *lifer*. It's who he was. He rinsed the dishes in the full sink, handing over the cups to each boy and Monica for drying.

"I'll put them away, okay?" She redried the cup Owen had given her, then stashed it in the upper cupboard.

He watched her fluid movements as he waited for Ethan and Owen to catch up on drying the dishes. Monica hadn't always moved with such grace. When he'd first laid eyes on her, she'd been awkward, with a good-sized nose and a habit of knocking things over. She grew in both height and composure as the years went by. She'd filled out some, her facial features softening. Monica now stood nearly three inches taller than him, still long and lean, but there was nothing awkward about her.

"What?" she asked.

He shrugged. "Nothing."

"Quit looking at me like that."

He laughed. "Like what?"

"I don't know, like I've got mustard on my chin or something."

He grinned. "Maybe I'd like mustard on your face."

She rolled her eyes. "Maybe you're crazy."

Maybe he was. He'd always kept a safe distance from Monica. She could never be called simply pretty. She'd grown up to be gorgeous and even more off-limits. Her brother would skin his hide if Cash ever hurt her. Living the way he did, in harm's way, he'd do exactly that. There were no guarantees that he wouldn't lose a limb or worse. No way did he ever want to saddle a woman with the kind of worry that came with his job. He liked the rush of adrenaline too much to ever quit, and he cared for his company far too much to get out.

Once the dishes were done and put away, Cash opened the slider to the back deck. "We've got to gather up some kindling to start the fire and green sticks to roast marshmallows."

"There are long metal forks around here somewhere," Monica offered.

Cash shook his head. "Sticks are way better."

"Yeah," Ethan agreed, again with a note of challenge in his voice. "Way better."

Monica threw up her hands in surrender. "Okay, sticks it is. Boys, if you have sweatshirts in your room, you'd best grab one. It's a little chilly outside."

Cash wasn't so sure about that, since the sun still felt warm to him, but it wasn't a bad idea. "You heard the lady. Grab your gear and I'll meet you outside."

The boys darted into their room.

"I'll bring out the stuff for s'mores, but I'm getting a jacket, too." Monica darted up the loft steps.

Cash grabbed matches and stepped outside. The crisp smell of fall was definitely in the air even though it was just the end of August. He gathered some dry branches and looked up as the back door slid open and Ethan and Owen came running toward him.

Monica was right behind them, carrying a tray loaded with everything needed to make s'mores and then some. He didn't remember ever putting peanut butter in the mix, but hey, why not? The late evening sunlight set her long blond hair aglow.

"You're doing it again." She elbowed him in the gut before setting the tray on a bench.

"What?" But he knew. He couldn't seem to stop drinking in every detail of her.

"We're going to need more kindling than that to start a fire." Monica headed into the woods, just beyond where the grass stopped.

The boys followed her.

Cash looked at the puny sticks he'd collected and chuckled. There were several cords for the fireplace stacked under the overhang at the side of the house, but Monica wanted to hunt for firewood. He dumped what he had in the firepit and joined them in search of better fuel.

Monica headed back to the firepit with her arms loaded with downed branches. She loved gathering wood for a campfire. Cash's nephews seemed to get into it, as well. Both Ethan's and Owen's arms were full. "Good job, guys."

"Can I light the fire?" Ethan asked.

Monica scrunched her nose. Not her call. "We'll have to ask your uncle Cash."

Uncle Cash.

She'd had no idea that Cassius William Miller would be so good with kids. He'd make a good family man, although as far as she knew, he'd never been close to getting married. He was thirty-four, but to her knowledge, Cash had never had a serious girlfriend. How come? He'd once joked that he was married to the marines, but evidently he'd been serious.

She dropped her wood just beyond the sandy circle surrounding the firepit that had been made from large rocks. "Boys, you can dump your wood here with mine. We have to stack it a certain way in the pit before we can light it."

"Yeah, we know. Our dad showed us plenty of times," Ethan said.

Monica bit her lip. She wanted to respond the right way, and ignoring that comment didn't seem like a good idea, so she probed a bit. "Did you have a lot of campfires with your dad?"

Ethan nodded with pride. "Yup. Even in the wintertime."

Monica glanced at Owen and her heart broke. His eyes appeared hopeful as he looked around. Did he understand that his father wasn't ever coming back?

Cash returned from the woods with his strong arms full of fallen branches.

Her attention drawn to the way his muscles bunched

and flexed as he broke up the pieces, Monica mumbled, "Well, your dad would be very proud that we're doing this tonight. Carrying on his tradition."

"What's that?" Ethan asked.

Looking away, Monica asked, "What's what?"

"A tra-di-shun?"

"It's something so special that you repeat it yearly, or even more, and think of someone or something special while you do. For example, at Christmas, my family always cuts down a fresh pine tree together. It's our tradition."

Ethan looked thoughtful. "Mom's allergic to pine trees so we can't do that."

Way to go. Monica looked to Cash for help. "Is there anything you can add about traditions?"

"Hmm, let me think a minute." He stroked his beard.

Monica made a big show of waiting for his answer by gesturing for him to get on with it.

It made the boys giggle.

Cash cast an aggravated look her way, which made the boys laugh even more, then he crouched down in front of them. "When your dad and I were your ages, we used to see who could spot the first star of the night."

"And then what?" Ethan asked, with hope shining in his eyes.

Cash looked at Monica. "The winner made a wish, but if he told what it was, it wouldn't come true. Come on, let's get this woodpile built up big so we can burn it."

"Yeah!" Ethan cheered.

Monica shook her head. Once a thrill seeker, always a thrill seeker. Cash did everything in a big way. Like now, turning a simple campfire into a huge bonfire. Growing up, he'd been the one who had often lured her brother Matthew into trouble or injury or both. Cash had always exhibited a need for speed, whether racing bicycles, motorbikes, snowmobiles or even cars. He still drove a muscle car. The black Dodge Challenger parked in front of the cabin might not be new, but it was no doubt fast. All the more reason to steer clear of Cash Miller. She had enough to worry about without the added concern that he'd one day break his neck.

She got busy stacking the gathered pieces of wood, leaning the smaller sticks against each other to form a tepee. She glanced at Owen watching her and stretched out her hand. "Want to help me?"

The boy nodded and inched closer.

"Let's lean those larger sticks over the smaller ones in the same shape, see?" Monica handed him a broken branch. "You try."

Owen handed it back to her.

Monica shrugged and anchored it against a larger one, then looked around. Cash and Ethan were hunting for green sticks for roasting the marshmallows.

Owen handed her another branch.

She smiled and searched those big gray eyes of his. Had he truly lost his ability to speak, or was he simply refusing to talk? When she was little, her older sister Cat used to hold her breath to get what she wanted. It rarely worked. Their mom refused to be manipulated. Owen looked much too sweet for such tactics, but then kids worked from a simpler approach than adults.

"Here we go. Four perfect sticks." Cash started stripping twigs and leaves off one.

Ethan copied his uncle with another stick.

"Owen, it looks like it's up to us to clean our own." Monica handed the five-year-old a stick.

He pulled at the leaves.

"Like this, Owen." Monica snapped off the little branches.

Owen followed suit and smiled.

"Good job." She looked up and caught Cash watching her.

His gaze softened and he mouthed *"Thank you."*

Monica nodded and returned to the task at hand. This might not be what she'd expected when she drove up here, but maybe God had saved her from the inevitable wallowing she would have sunk into had she been here all by herself. Maybe tonight was a good thing, something she needed, because her mind was drifting away from her own issues to why Owen wasn't talking.

Cash sat back and watched Monica help both Ethan and Owen roast their marshmallows. The fire had burned down some. The boys had loved the towering flames shooting high into the sky. They'd jumped up and down. Ethan had cheered. Cash had loved it, too, regardless of the indulgent smile Monica had given him, as if he should know better.

Yup, she'd make a good mom. He couldn't believe she wasn't already married. Her brother said she'd dated some, but never anything serious. He wondered why. He'd wondered a lot of things about Monica over the years. She'd occasionally slipped into his thoughts at the oddest, least opportune times, like during a lull in gunfire, but he'd firmly pushed her aside. That was a good way to get killed, losing focus on the mission at hand over something as simple as a woman back home.

He glanced toward where the sun had set, leaving behind a sky that glowed orange and pink through a clearing in the trees. It was only eight forty, less than an hour before bedtime for the boys.

That would put him alone with Monica—

"There's the first star, Uncle Cash." Ethan pointed to the darkening sky just above the clearing.

"That's Venus, buddy. Not a star at all, but a planet."

The kid's eyes narrowed as if he didn't quite believe him. "Can I still make a wish?"

Cash chuckled. "Sure. Or you can wait a little bit longer for the stars to pop out. Then it's off to bed."

Ethan groaned. "Do we have to?"

Cash looked over at Owen, slouching low in the camp chair. His eyelids drooped. "Afraid so, buddy. Big day tomorrow."

"What about Dogman? Will he come out after we're in bed?"

Owen's eyes flew open, wide as half-dollars.

"No, Ethan. There's no such thing as Dogman. He's make-believe, only a pretend character in an old story. Stop trying to scare your brother."

Ethan folded his arms and pouted.

Owen slipped out of the camp chair and climbed onto Monica's lap.

She welcomed him, wrapping her arms around his waist, then resting her chin on the top of his head. "Owen, did you want to make a wish?"

He shook his head.

"Why not, little dude?" Cash asked, hoping Owen might answer with spoken words. It was why he'd brought the boys to this cabin, hoping a change of scenery and lots of activity might reopen the floodgates of his speech.

He shrugged instead, leaning deeper into Monica's arms.

"I'll wish for us, okay, Owen?" Ethan whispered.

Cash battled against the knot that formed in his throat. Why had he told the boys that stupid tradition of wishing on stars? He knew what they wished for—something that couldn't come true. They wanted their dad back.

Cash wished for the same thing. He'd never had the chance to tell Cole how much he admired him or how much he loved him. There hadn't been a proper goodbye the last time he'd seen him. They'd slapped each other's backs, saying they'd see each other later, but later never came. He caught Monica's watery-eyed gaze across the crackling campfire and nearly lost it.

Why did his brother have to die? He had a wife and two boys to look after. Cash had been the one dancing with death for as long as he could remember. All those deployments and risky missions into enemy territories had left him whole, without critical injury. Why?

Why was life so unfair?

They sat silently by the fire and Cash stared into the flames. When he finally checked his watch, it was well past nine. He glanced at Monica, still holding Owen, who'd fallen asleep.

He stood and reached for the boy. "Time for bed."

Ethan got up without argument.

Cash shifted Owen to his shoulder and followed Ethan inside.

Monica stayed put by the fire.

"Go to the bathroom, Ethan." Cash didn't bother with orders to brush teeth. This was camp and normal grooming habits were pretty much ignored. It's what made it *camp*.

He entered the bedroom the boys shared and laid Owen on the bottom bunk. He didn't want to wake him, so Cash just slipped off the boy's shoes and socks before lifting the covers over his motionless form, still dressed in his sweatshirt and jeans.

Ethan came in, changed into his pajamas, and climbed up to the top bunk. "Uncle Cash?"

"Yeah, bud?"

"Is she staying the whole time?"

"Monica? I don't know. If she does, is that okay with you?"

"Yeah." Ethan nodded. "Owen likes her, and then Mom and Grandma can meet her, too."

"She's easy to like." Cash ruffled the kid's hair.

No matter how much Ethan teased his little brother, he still looked out for him. He was a lot like his father in that respect. "Your dad would be proud of how you're taking care of your little brother."

Ethan looked at him hard. "I wish he was here."

That knot deep in Cash's throat tightened up again, but he swallowed through it. "Me, too, buddy. Good night, Ethan. I love you."

Ethan looked at him, appearing wiser than his tender years. "I love you, too."

Cash closed the door only halfway, leaving the bathroom light on. He padded into the kitchen, opened the fridge and grabbed a couple cold beverages before heading back out to the fire.

Monica looked up as he approached.

He handed her a can. "Want one?"

"Sure." She snapped open the tab top and took a sip. "So, what's the story with your nephews?"

"My sister-in-law was at her wit's end with Owen not speaking. Since I had the time, I figured I'd try to help. Ruth had some legal stuff with the tree business, so I asked to bring the boys here. The timing worked well."

"He'll talk eventually, won't he?"

"I hope so. I think it's the stress of losing his dad. I've seen soldiers psychologically lose their eyesight, even their hearing, after combat, with nothing physically wrong with them. If Owen is purposefully keeping quiet, I imagine he'll give up eventually. I'm hoping some activity away from home will flip the talking switch back on."

Monica's eyes shone with approval. "It's good of you to try."

Cash shrugged and looked away. "They're my brother's boys. I have to do something."

Monica nodded. "How's your mom?"

His mother had told him that he was all she had left now, and that comment stuck with him, haunting him. He shrugged. "Upset. She moved in with Cole a while back, after she sold the house."

"That's good." Monica shivered and pulled her chair closer to the fire.

"I can throw on a couple more logs."

"No. It's fine. I'm going to turn in soon."

He watched her stare at the flames, admiring her profile. She still had a long nose, but it was straight. He'd thought for sure that he'd broken it once during a snowball fight when he'd hit her dead-on, but she'd kept a stiff upper lip.

She'd always come back with a sharp retort to his

teasing. He liked that about Monica. She'd never been a wimp. She had a stubborn streak and didn't like to show any weakness. More tomboy than princess, her choice of swanky clothes and makeup seemed at odds with the girl he'd grown up with. But then again, maybe he held onto his youthful memories of Monica too tightly because he didn't want to notice how beautiful she'd become nor accept how attractive he found her.

Tipping his head, he asked, "Why'd you come up here alone?"

"Just needed to get away for a few days." She took another sip, but didn't glance up from the fire.

"Everything okay back home?"

"Everyone's fine."

"But not you?"

She looked at him with those expressive blue eyes of hers reflecting anguish. "I've got some decisions to make."

"Ahh. Is there a guy involved?"

She uttered a short bark of laughter. "Not anymore. He broke it off. We weren't serious or anything."

It was Cash's turn to chuckle at the cavalier tone in her voice. "Monica, Monica, Monica. What'd you do?"

Her face turned grim. "Absolutely nothing."

"And yet he broke it off—"

"It's fine," she interrupted. "I'm not in a good place for a relationship, anyway."

He leaned forward, curious. "Why not?"

She finished her drink and crumpled the can, then stood. "Not something I really want to talk about, either."

Warning bells went off inside his brain. Monica wasn't one to hide anything. Worse, where was that sharp tongue of hers? She looked defeated and that wasn't at all like her.

Cash tried again. "If you do want to talk about it, I can listen."

She patted his shoulder. "I know you can. Thanks."

He grabbed her hand and gave it a friendly squeeze.

She surprised him by hanging on tight. "Good night, Cash."

"See you in the morning. I hope you stick around for breakfast. I make pretty mean pancakes."

She let go of his hand. "I wouldn't miss it."

"Good." He listened as she made her way inside the cabin, closing the slider door with a whoosh.

He stayed by the fire, watching the low flames awhile longer. He'd do what he could to convince Monica to stay on for a bit. Cash needed her help, and maybe she needed them, to give her mind a rest from whatever decisions she faced.

He wouldn't pry into her situation, but he'd pray for her. He'd been praying a lot lately when he wasn't yelling at God for taking yet another person he cared about from him. As for Monica, he shouldn't know too much and it'd be better if she didn't tell him. He was leaving soon, so he didn't want any entanglements with a woman back home. Getting too close wouldn't work for him. It might cost him his edge.

Chapter Three

Upstairs in the loft, Monica changed into a pair of pajama bottoms and a plain T-shirt. The warmth of the day had given way to a chilly night, but they hadn't built a fire in the woodstove. There wasn't any point, since tomorrow promised to be much warmer according to the weather forecast. Propping pillows against the headboard of the bed, she slipped under the covers and grabbed her phone.

Her brother had texted her back saying that he'd given Cash the keys to the cabin before he caught ship. He added that he was sorry he couldn't join them, because it would have been like old times.

Monica felt a reminiscent stab to her heart and texted back that she wished he was here, too. Of all her brothers, she'd been closest to Matthew. Growing up, she'd idolized him and tagged along as often as she could. More times than not that meant hanging around Cash, too.

Cash had been the one to teach her to drive a snowmobile on one such outing. She'd been only thirteen and wanted to go with them. A trailhead was right down the road from her parents' house. Cash had chosen the two-up so she could ride with him, much to her brother's chagrin. Matthew hadn't wanted her to go, because the two of them loved jumping ditches and riding off trail.

While Matthew was way ahead on his sled, Cash had pulled over to let her drive. She'd never forget the thrill of it, her first time driving a snowmobile. She'd been afraid, too, but Cash had been right behind her, coaching her on how to steer, showing her how to brake and speed up.

His gloved hands had covered hers a few times through the curves in the winding trail. She smiled, even now remembering the feel of his strong arms around her, guiding her.

Matthew had had a fit when they'd finally caught up to him. She'd been too young to operate a snow machine without a safety certificate, and the guys, at only seventeen, were too young to legally supervise her. Fortunately, they hadn't been caught by the authorities. It had been midweek and the Department of Natural Resources officers were typically out in full force on weekends.

Now that she thought about it, she realized Cash had often taken the time to teach her things, as if she was his little sister, too. She owed the precision of her foul shots in basketball to his coaching. She couldn't even count the times he'd shot baskets with her before leaving the Zelinsky household for his own home in town.

She wanted to help him with his nephews, but wasn't sure how. Still holding her phone, she searched the internet for information regarding children and grief. So far, much of what she'd found dealt with how to tell kids when a loved one died. She kept searching.

After an hour of perusing various sites, she was

amazed by what she'd found. There in print was Owen's manifestation of grief by not talking. He might be a little old by a couple of years for the loss of speech, according to the article, but still, it was all there and it didn't sound abnormal. So there was hope. Obviously, their mother must have thought so, or Monica doubted she would have sent her boys with Cash to the cabin.

Cash.

He wanted to help his nephews, but Cash was grieving, too. He had that same determined look in his eyes that she'd seen when his father had passed away. He'd been determined to beat his sorrow then by sheer force of will, fighting for control through the funeral without shedding a tear.

Monica had been twelve at the time and Cash sixteen. She remembered it well, because that was when she'd first looked at Cash with new eyes. He wasn't her brother's annoying friend anymore, but her friend, too. Maybe a little more than friends, because that was the day hugging Cash Miller in an attempt to console him had seemed to move him into a special place in her heart.

Her phone whistled with an incoming text, scattering her thoughts. Scanning the screen, she opened a message from her mom.

Are you okay?

Of course her mother would check on her, but it was too late to call, with the boys in bed. Monica didn't want her voice to carry and wake them up. She quickly texted back that she was fine and she wasn't alone. She explained that Cash was here with his two young nephews.

After a couple seconds, another text came through.

Good. I'm glad you're not alone. Have some FUN and give him our love.

Always to the point, her mother. Monica smiled as she texted back. I will. Love you.

Just then she heard the downstairs slider door open and close. Cash had come in from the fire and Monica listened to his footsteps on the hardwood floors below. He stopped at the fridge, opened it and then closed it. Next, she heard the snap of a tab top can being opened.

She closed her eyes and listened harder. It sounded like he was in the living room, right below her. If she got out of bed and looked down over the railing, she'd see him. Would he see her? Was he maybe gazing up at the loft right now?

Her heart skipped a few beats, but Monica reined in her foolish thoughts before they got out of hand. She might still harbor her childhood crush for Cash, but that's all it was or ever could be. Their lives had veered in completely different directions. His was wrapped around the 2nd Marine Raider Battalion based in North Carolina, while hers was here in Michigan.

His footsteps sounded lighter and farther away and then she heard the soft click of his bedroom door being shut. Monica let out the breath she'd been holding. She had so many memories of him, memories of the two of them growing up, and they came to her like a silent film-strip, making her smile and filling her with warmth. The words she'd said in jest while they were making dinner were absolutely true.

Cash Miller is dangerous.

She was far too vulnerable right now and her emotions too raw to entertain any ideas about her attraction to Cash. She didn't want to drag him into her troubles when he had his own to deal with. In the morning, after breakfast, she'd pack up and head home. That'd be the right thing to do. The smart thing.

The next morning, Cash struck a match and held it to the pile of kindling in the woodstove. Watching the flames quickly spread, he threw in a couple small logs before shutting the glass doors. That would take the chill out of the cabin.

He gazed out the windows to where the sky was getting lighter, ready to meet the rising sun. Mist huddled in low spots and the grass glistened with heavy dew. He'd always been an early riser. Something about the stillness of early morning appealed to him. Everything seemed peaceful at the start of the day, before plans and missions unfolded.

He wasn't at peace, though. Deep inside, he still raged at God for taking his brother. God was big enough to handle his anger, he knew that, but it didn't help answer one simple question. Why would God take Cole? What purpose could it possibly serve to leave those two boys without a father?

He'd chased that question round and round and still came up empty. When a soldier died, Cash could accept it, even though it was painful. Even after his commanding officer had died in his arms, he knew that going into harm's way, death was part of the deal. Losing his brother to some freak accident wasn't.

Rubbing his whisker-covered chin, he stuffed all that into a proverbial box to look at later or never. Rehashing the past didn't change it. Besides, he had breakfast to make. He entered the kitchen area and quietly mixed the ingredients for chocolate chip pancakes. Letting the batter sit, he made coffee.

He spotted Monica making her way down the loft steps dressed in a sweatshirt over a pair of Detroit Lions flannel pajama bottoms. Her stick-straight hair hadn't been brushed and her eyes seemed a little puffy, but she still managed to look good. Maybe too good. He'd always preferred her natural good looks to all that makeup, anyway.

"Morning." The raw sound in his voice wasn't welcome.

She yawned as if still half-asleep. "Is that coffee ready?"

In spite of the boxed-up rage over Cole's death and noticing Monica far more than he should, he forced a smile. "Not yet."

"Are the boys up?" She sat on a bar stool across from him at the kitchen island and hung her head in her hands, as if trying to wipe away the remnants of sleep still clinging to her.

"Not yet."

"Well, aren't you a chatty one this morning. What are you doing?"

"Pancakes." He gave her an insolent grin. Mornings weren't meant for a lot of talk.

She yawned again. "How'd you sleep?"

"Better than you, it appears."

She shrugged. "I'm not a morning person."

He chuckled. "So I see."

She made a face as she slipped off the stool, grabbed a mug from the cupboard and pulled the coffeepot off its hot plate.

"It's not done brewing."

"So? It has auto pause."

Cash spread his arms wide. "So…you'll make the rest of the pot weak."

She shrugged, opened the fridge and grabbed the half and half, drizzling a good portion of it into her mug. "It's only one cup."

"Monica, Monica, Monica." He watched her take a sip and grimace. "Too strong, huh? I told you."

Again she made a face as she grabbed the sugar dispenser with a stainless steel top, tipped it over and poured a healthy dose into her cup. Then she grabbed his measuring spoons and stirred.

"Give me those." He reached for the spoons at the same time she was pushing them his way, and his hand covered hers. He didn't let go.

Her eyes found his. "What?"

"Are you always this annoying?"

Monica pulled her hand back. "I could say the same about you."

Of course she could. He'd teased her since they were kids. "Are you going to stay the weekend?"

"I figured I'd leave after breakfast."

Disappointment stabbed him quick and hard. He didn't like that feeling, either. "I'm taking the boys out on the side-by-sides. It'd be more fun if you drove one, too."

She frowned, making tiny lines appear above her nose and along her brow line. Even her eyebrows were perfectly shaped.

His gaze swept to her flawlessly painted orange fingertips. Monica had become a woman who took meticulous care of her appearance. His buddies would call that high maintenance, but he knew Monica well enough to know that wasn't so. She'd always held her own in any activity he and her brothers had dragged her into. So why'd he get the feeling that perfection in her appearance might be a shield?

"Do you know how to drive a utility vehicle?" he asked.

She looked insulted, reinforcing what he already knew. Monica was no shrinking violet. "Of course I know how to drive one."

She still hadn't accepted his offer to stay. It might be smarter if she left, but Cash had meant that prayer. He needed help, so he pleaded. A little. "Owen is drawn to you, Monica. You might be the key that unlocks his speech."

Her bright blue eyes turned stormy and dark. Her lashes were lighter without makeup and looked as if they'd been dipped in gold. His fingers itched to reach out and touch to see if any of that gold dust came off.

Monica had taken a deep breath, as if rallying her courage, when a horrible cry sounded from the boys' room.

Nightmare?

Cash nodded toward the sound. "I better check that out. Ethan sometimes has bad dreams."

Monica nodded.

He dreaded this. His sister-in-law had warned him about the dreams, which had become worse since Cole died, but so far Cash hadn't had to deal with one. Taking a deep breath, he pushed open the door to the boys' room.

Ethan jerked awake. "Dad?"

"It's me, Ethan. Uncle Cash." He crept toward the beds. Ethan was on the top bunk.

The kid recognized him with such a sorrowful look of disappointment that Cash's heart broke. Then the waterworks started. Silent at first, then louder. Deep wails of pain.

Cash pulled him from the bed, ready to take him out so he wouldn't wake Owen, but it was too late. Owen woke up, took in the scene and started crying, too.

"I know, buddy, I know." Cash sat in a chair near the bottom bunk, shifting Ethan to his lap. The kid was all arms and legs, but he rested his head on Cash's shoulder and bawled.

A lump the size of a tank stuck in his throat as he reached for Owen.

The little guy climbed into his lap in turn, hanging on for dear life.

Cash closed his eyes and swallowed hard, trying to keep it together. He hadn't cried in years and he wasn't going to start now. He felt a light touch on his shoulder and looked up into Monica's concerned eyes.

She gave his shoulder a squeeze but didn't let go.

That small gesture of comfort nearly undid him. He leaned his head against her arm and turned so his lips grazed her wrist as he whispered, "Don't leave."

She sniffed, knelt down and wrapped her arms around all three of them.

Monica held on tight, tighter even. She fought against the tears that threatened by closing her eyes. She couldn't erase that look of helpless devastation in Cash's eyes from her mind, though. Even worse, her skin tingled from that brief touch of his lips.

This wasn't good at all. She felt like the pile of dry tinder in the box next to the woodstove. One embrace from Cash and she'd go up in flames, burning them both. She needed to leave as soon as possible, and yet he needed her help. He'd practically begged her to stay, and those boys might need her help, too. She had all that information she'd found online.

Monica pulled away. This was too intense. Leaning back on her haunches, she said, "I don't know about you guys, but I'm hungry for those pancakes Uncle Cash is making."

Owen slipped off his uncle's knee, eyes wide.

Even Ethan moved back, rubbing the tears from his eyes. "What kind?"

Cash sent her a look of pure gratitude before answering, "Chocolate chip."

"Yes-s-s!" Ethan fist pumped the air.

"Maybe you two should go wash up and then meet us in the kitchen," Monica offered.

The boys raced for the bathroom, shoving each other, tears forgotten.

She glanced at Cash. "You okay?"

He slapped the tops of his jean-clad thighs and stood. "Yeah. I don't know how they shift gears so fast. Sad one minute and then laughing the next."

"Kids are pretty resilient that way." Monica followed him to the kitchen. The boys were still horsing around in the bathroom. She heard the water running in the sink and hoped they were washing their hands.

Keeping her voice low, she added, "Don't worry, that's normal. In fact, last night I looked up information on grieving kids, and Owen's situation is not uncommon, either."

"Yeah?" Cash's whole face lit up.

"Yeah."

The boys tore out of the bathroom, racing to the bar

stools at the island. They each climbed onto one, then kept jockeying each other, as if trying to knock the other off.

"Boys, cool it," Cash said.

Monica saw Ethan pinch his little brother. Owen kicked him in return, but they'd quieted. She shook her head.

The coffee was done, so she dumped her first cup in the sink and poured a fresh one. "Cash, do you want coffee?"

"Please." His voice sounded soft.

She felt him nearby. He stood right behind her and her whole body tensed.

He reached over her shoulder into the cupboard and grabbed a mug. "No cream or sugar."

"You're hard-core." Her own voice sounded strained.

He gave her a lopsided grin. "Marines don't take it easy. Now get out of my space so I can make breakfast."

Monica joined the boys on a bar stool, but watched as Cash grabbed plates, silverware and glasses, which he placed in front of them while the griddle pan heated on the stove.

Really, she should do something. "Want me to get the milk and syrup?"

He waved her offer away. "I got it. Just sit."

She sipped her coffee, which she'd laced with cream and sugar. In spite of sneaking an early cup before it had finished brewing, the coffee was still strong. Evidently Cash liked his java close to battery acid.

She couldn't pretend she didn't enjoy being waited on, especially watching Cash do so. Maybe she should test him, ask him to grab a bunch of stuff for her, to see what he'd do. Just for fun. Tempting, but then he might burn the pancakes. It wasn't worth the risk.

Thinking about fun, she recalled how her mother's text last night had told her to have some. Monica knew riding those two side-by-sides would be that and more.

Ethan banged his silverware on the island counter and started to chant, "Pancakes, pancakes…"

Owen joined in, banging his silverware. He didn't speak.

Monica was about to tell the boys to stop, but didn't. They weren't hurting anything other than her ears.

Cash didn't seem bothered by the noise, either, as he ladled batter into eight puddles on the griddle. He sprinkled in mini chocolate chips and waited until the batter bubbled. Then he made a big show of flipping the pancakes over with a spatula.

Monica clapped and so did the boys.

He turned off the burners and fetched milk, maple syrup and a dish of butter, which he then placed on the island before serving the pancakes.

Monica helped Owen with the syrup, happy to see that it was from her parents' sugar shack. Then she filled his glass with milk, while Cash helped Ethan. Their gazes met over the boys' heads and held. She read the message he sent loud and clear.

He wanted her to stay.

Tempted, Monica looked away.

Everyone quieted as they ate, digging into the fluffy cakes dotted with melted, gooey chocolate.

Monica broke the silence. "These are really good."

"Want more?"

"No. Thanks." She patted her midsection. He'd made

four large pancakes each for them and four smaller ones for the boys. She'd gotten her fill and then some.

"How about you, Ethan? Owen?"

Both boys shook their heads, their mouths full. Owen had chocolate smeared on one chubby cheek.

After Ethan downed his last bite, followed by a long gulp of milk, he wiped his mouth with his sleeve. "What are we going to do today?"

Again Cash glanced her way. "Well, I was thinking of taking the side-by-sides out for a spin."

Ethan looked confused.

"Four-wheelers, UTVs—whatever you want to call them."

"Really?" The boy's golden eyes gleamed as he turned to Monica. "Are you going with us?"

Torn, she remained silent.

"Monica?" Cash's gray eyes coaxed her before he turned to the five-year-old. "How 'bout you, Owen? Want to go four-wheeling?"

Owen nodded, even though he didn't look like he understood what that meant. The little boy slipped his hand into hers and tugged.

Monica knew what the kid was trying to do and her resolve to leave shredded. Glancing at the three of them waiting for an answer, she felt her heart pounding a little harder.

She wanted to stay, oh, how she wanted to, but… Rationalization came quickly. What was one weekend? She needed some fun—hadn't her mother said so? She'd stay today and tonight and then leave tomorrow morning. No big deal. As long as she kept her cool and her heart safe, it'd be fine.

Taking a deep breath and letting it back out with a

loud whoosh that made the boys laugh, Monica officially caved in. "Okay, I'll stay on one condition."

Three pairs of male eyes narrowed.

Monica nearly burst out laughing at the wary expression they had in common.

Cash and his nephews certainly looked related. Like family.

"And the condition is?" Cash asked.

"We color when we get back."

He looked completely confused. "Color?"

"Paper and crayons or colored pencils." In her internet search for tips to help grieving kids, she'd found a couple drawing exercises to try. It was one way of getting them to express their feelings and start the conversation by letting some of that grief out on paper. It might help.

If she was going to stay, she was going to help them, including Cash. Especially Cash.

"Okay, we can color, right, boys?" Cash nodded.

"Right," Ethan agreed.

Owen simply nodded.

"Okay, then I'll stay." Monica grinned.

The boys cheered and Cash gave her a grateful smile.

It felt good to please them, but it would feel even better to help them. Really help. She hoped this coloring exercise would do that. She also hoped it didn't backfire on her, because she had some grief of her own to deal with.

Chapter Four

After the dishes were done and the kitchen cleaned, Cash clapped his hands. "Okay, boys, let's get ready to ride. Long pants and long sleeves."

He watched the two scurry away to get dressed, making as much noise as possible—pretty amazing considering Owen didn't speak. But he stomped. Cash glanced at Monica, who was still ruminating over a cup of coffee. Her eyes had a faraway look and were sort of glazed over. "You okay?"

She snapped back to the present. "Yeah, why?"

He narrowed his gaze. "You were miles away just now."

"Are you sure this is a good idea, with the boys on the side-by-sides? Owen is so young."

"Your uncle has a bump seat for young kids. I already installed it."

Monica didn't quite look convinced. "What about Ethan?"

"I think he's big enough to be buckled in the passenger seat. He's pretty tall for an eight-year-old."

"He must get that from his mother's side." Monica peeked over the rim of her cup.

Cash liked the teasing glint in her eyes. This was his Monica, the one he remembered well. Wait—since when had he started thinking of her as *his*? He mentally pushed aside possessive thoughts that could only lead to trouble, and grinned. "We can't all be storks."

The mischievous look remained in her eyes as she took her last sip of coffee, got up and put her mug in the sink. "Low-to-the-ground birds are important, too."

He laughed outright at her jab about his shorter stature. "You wound me."

"I highly doubt it." She stood. "I'm going to go change."

"Hmm, too bad."

She turned on him. "Why?"

"I like those Detroit Lions pj's." He winked and enjoyed the rash of color that spread up her neck to her cheeks.

She rallied, snapping sarcastically, "I bet you say that to all the girls."

"Nope, just you." Cash realized the minute he said it that he was serious. Sure, he'd had his share of flirtations and the like, but there'd always been something special about Monica. Something different, but also scary as if staring over the edge of a steep cliff.

The air turned heavy with awareness as they stood staring at each other for a few beats of the heart. The boys chose that moment to run back into the living room, chasing each other. Owen had his brother's shoe.

"Give it back," Ethan yelled.

Owen squealed and kept running.

Cash caught the little redhead. "Whoa, give him his tennis shoe."

Owen shook his head and pointed at his brother.

Cash tried to figure out what Ethan had taken from Owen to start the feud, but came up empty. He spotted Monica slipping upstairs, and closed his eyes for a brief second. He needed to clear his mind from the sticky cobwebs of connection that she'd spun. Focusing back on the boys, he called his nephews to order, using his military voice. The one that broached no argument. "Cool it. Both of you."

That got their attention. Owen dropped the shoe and Ethan's eyes widened.

More quietly, Cash said, "Let's get shoes on or we don't have to go."

Ethan looked like he was weighing his options, maybe even wondering if Cash would follow through on that threat to stay home. After a moment's consideration, he yelled, "But it's his fault."

"Doesn't matter. I'll take care of Owen." At the look of pure frustration on Ethan's face, Cash softened. "Go on. Get ready."

In a huff, Ethan bent to pick up his tennis shoe, then ran back to his room.

When they were alone, Cash bent down on one knee so he was closer to eye level with Owen. "Why'd you take your brother's shoe?"

The little boy shook his head. He wasn't giving up anything.

Cash blew out his breath. "Finish getting ready."

Owen didn't move, but pointed to the loft.

Cash smiled. "Monica is going with us."

Owen gave him a telling look.

"You want to ride with her?"

He nodded.

Cash chuckled. "Of course, Owen. No sweat. Go get your shoes on."

The little boy tore into his room.

Cash heard Ethan ask Owen why he'd gotten him in trouble, but the question was met with silence. Cash shook his head. Those two boys were like him and their father at that age—always arguing, but also close.

Already dressed himself, Cash fetched a light wind-breaker and made sure the boys each had theirs. Then he waited for Monica.

Monica leaned against the upstairs bathroom door. Her racing pulse was finally slowing down to normal. These prickly feelings were no joke. Cash made her want things she couldn't have, things she might never be able to have.

Closing her eyes to keep the sudden tears at bay, Monica blew out her breath. All this drama was ridiculous. She was emotionally vulnerable, overreactive, and Cash was simply being his usual caring self. That was all. Surely, his feelings didn't run any deeper than any longtime friend.

"Hey, you going to take all day or what?" His voice carried up from below.

She tamped down the sudden irritation his impatience roused and tried for a civil response. "Hold your horses."

"Daylight is burning."

Ha! So much for his caring self.

"Give me a few minutes." Rolling her eyes, she entered the bathroom.

Quickly, she brushed her teeth, then secured her hair

in a long ponytail before changing into jeans. Applying a swipe of peach-colored lip balm, she looked in the mirror and crinkled her nose. Definitely not her best look by any means, but it would have to do. No shower or makeup was unusual for her, but there was no point even if she had time. They were hitting four-wheeler trails that were dirty.

And Cash would no doubt drive too fast.

Monica squared her shoulders. There was nothing new about the attraction she had for Cash Miller. Like always, once they went their separate ways, it would fizzle and die. Out of sight, out of mind, and she'd be out of sight by tomorrow.

"Monica, are you coming or what?" His deep voice boomed again.

After grabbing an old windbreaker from one of the dressers in the loft, she charged down the stairs. Coming to a quick stop on the last step, she teetered over Cash, who stood at the bottom.

His gaze swept her from head to toe. "'Bout time. What about shoes?"

Monica wiggled one bare foot, flashing her peach-painted toenails. With a pair of socks in hand, she nudged by him. "There are rubber boots in the closet down here."

"You expecting a flood?"

"There's always mud out there and the forecast on my phone predicts rain later." Slipping her feet into the boots, she looked around. "Where are the boys?"

"Outside. It's going to be a warm one today."

"Good. More fun that way." She stopped to grab her purse, then gazed about once again.

"What are you looking for now?"

She shrugged. "Do we have everything we need? Phones, first aid? Water?"

He tipped his head. "You're going to question a marine if he's ready to roll?"

Of course he'd have everything loaded and ready by the time she got down here. Monica smiled. "I guess I should know better, huh?"

"Yeah, you should." He held the door for her, then tugged her ponytail as she walked by.

She turned on him with a challenging grin. "Do that again and you'll be sorry."

He pulled her hair again and laughed. "I like living on the edge."

Monica gave him a mock punch to the arm. "Just remember we have two kids on that edge today. Not too fast, okay?"

That sobered him quickly. "I'm careful with them."

"But not if it's just you, right?" She didn't really know what his military life was like, but knowing him, suspected he'd charge in without a thought to his own safety. Her brother Matthew had seen some of Cash's commendations and medals.

He didn't answer. In fact, he looked annoyed with the question. "Let's just go."

Taking in his faded red T-shirt with the words *Semper Fi* across the front, Monica got the sinking feeling that he'd always be a marine. She followed him toward the two-seater utility vehicles parked in the pole barn.

"This is awesome." Ethan caught up with them.

Owen was staring at something in the grass.

Monica stepped close to the younger boy and tried to figure out what had captured his interest. A woolly bear caterpillar inched across a dirt patch. "What is it?"

Owen looked up and then pointed.

Monica tried again, hoping he'd answer. "What is that?"

He dropped his head and let his shoulders droop.

She chuckled at the little boy's body language, which clearly said she was a dunce for not knowing a caterpillar when she saw one. She bent down and placed her finger on the ground in front of the fuzzy, black and rust colored creature. Once it crawled onto her skin, she lifted her hand so Owen could see it up close.

"Uh, could you play with bugs later?" Cash stood over them, looking grim.

Monica held up the caterpillar. "It's not just any bug. Woolly bears are special. They predict the upcoming winter, isn't that right, Owen?"

The boy nodded, but remained silent.

Cash's gray eyes softened. "What's that one have to say?"

Monica studied the little caterpillar making its way across her palm toward her wrist and tried to remember what she'd read about them. "There's a lot of rust on this little guy, so I think that means a milder winter."

"You never were prissy." Cash smiled.

Monica set the caterpillar back on the ground, then watched it inch away for a few seconds before she stood up. "Couldn't be, with seven brothers."

"No, I suppose not."

She tipped her head. "When did you get the cabin keys from Matthew?"

"He came up for Cole's funeral and offered them to me in case I needed to get away. Good thing I had the cabin to go to, considering." Cash nodded toward Owen.

"Yeah, that worked out well." She studied him.

Cash's emotions were well hidden. No sorrow lurked in his clear gray eyes. In fact, he had his game face on, the one he wore when looking for adventure. "Come on. Let's get helmets on these boys and head out."

Now wasn't the time to talk about loss. Monica offered Owen her hand and they followed Cash into the pole barn, where all the recreation gear was hung up or shelved. Selecting child-sized helmets and goggles amid the stash of adult ones wasn't easy, but thankfully, they found some small sizes that fit Cash's nephews pretty well.

"Here we go, Owen. I think these will do nicely." The kid looked adorable.

Fastening the helmet strap under Owen's chin, Monica wondered how often Cash came back to see his mom at his brother's place here in the UP. Monica remembered when Mrs. Miller sold the family home in Maple Springs. Cash had grown up there, in town. Did he ever miss it? Probably not, since he rarely visited their hometown.

She watched as Ethan climbed into the passenger seat and Cash buckled him in. The boy's feet didn't quite reach the floor, but came pretty close. Close enough.

"Ready, Owen? You're going to sit real close to Monica, you fortunate little fella." Cash gave her a wink.

Even though she knew he was teasing, Monica felt her heart give a little skip. She watched as he lifted Owen into the bumper seat placed between the driver's and passenger's, and buckled him in tight.

"You didn't need me to stay and drive. With that middle seat, you could have taken one side-by-side with both boys."

"Yeah, but then you'd have missed out on all the fun."

That was true. Monica looked forward to this. She looked forward to fun. "How far are we going?"

Cash gave her a wicked grin. "Until we stop."

She took a deep breath. He'd better not go too fast. She slipped behind the wheel, pulled on her goggles and started the engine. The utility vehicle hummed to life and so did she. Blood pumped quickly through her veins as they rolled out into the woods.

"Go faster!" Ethan hollered.

Cash glanced in the side mirror, glad to see that Monica kept pace beyond the cloud of dust left by his machine. These things went only so fast, but he'd test that.

Seeing a straightaway up ahead, he pushed down on the gas and they pulled away from the other vehicle.

"Yes-s-s!" Ethan held on tight.

Cash checked the speedometer and gave it a little more. Rounding a slight curve in the trail, he floored the engine in order to hit a narrow creek at full throttle. With a whoosh, shallow water splashed up the sides of the UTV and over the roof before flooding the floorboard.

He slowed down and pulled off the trail, turning around so they could watch Monica's side-by-side go through the same creek bed.

"That was awesome." Ethan grinned.

Water droplets fell from the roof. Cash looked down at his feet, which were soaked, along with his jeans, and grinned. "Did you get wet?"

Ethan nodded. "It was great."

Cash laughed. The temperature had been climbing throughout the morning and now it was hot. The cool dousing actually felt good.

He heard Monica's side-by-side coming and was pleased when she sped up to cross the creek, spraying water in all directions.

When she pulled over, Owen was laughing. Monica's smile was big, too, as she yelled out, "That was fun. You guys were flying."

Relieved that she wasn't going to lecture him on going too fast, Cash killed the engine and got out. This seemed like a good spot to take a break.

Monica shut off her vehicle, as well. She unbuckled Owen and lifted him to the ground, then got out, showing off her dry feet. "These boots came in handy."

"Good call." He nodded and opened the cooler strapped on the back of his utility vehicle. "Water?"

Monica slipped her goggles atop her head and reached for the bottled water like a desperate woman. "Please."

He watched as she dampened a bandanna she pulled from her pocket, then wiped her face with it. He chuckled at her preening. Her face was only going to get dirty again. "You kept up pretty good."

"Not in that straightaway. How fast were you going?"

He shrugged and braced for her scolding. "As fast as it would go."

Her eyes widened. "Cash…"

He held up his hand. "These things go only so fast, and as you can see, we did just fine."

Ethan chugged his water and burped. "It was awesome."

Monica shifted her gaze from him to the boy and then back. She shook her head as if Cash was a lost cause.

Maybe he was. He'd always tested boundaries and pushed against restrictions. That trait had served him well in the field. It's why he'd been recommended for MARSOC.

She looked around. "Where to now?"

Cash downed his water and tossed the empty bottle back in the cooler. "Someplace for lunch."

The boys jumped up and down, and Ethan asked, "Can we get pizza?"

Cash chuckled. "I don't know. We'll have to see what they have."

Monica finished her water, too. "Do you know where to go?"

"There's a restaurant right off the trail north of here. We used to go there when we were snowmobiling. Good food, too." It had been a while since he'd been there and he hoped it was still open.

Monica smiled. "Fine, because I'm getting hungry."

"Me, too." He turned to the boys, who were kicking their water bottles along the ground. "Toss those into the cooler and let's go."

Owen pointed to the nearby woods.

"What is it, Owen?" Cash wished he would speak already.

The five-year-old shifted from foot to foot and then grabbed at his zipper.

Cash said to Ethan, "Take your brother toward those woods so he can go to the bathroom. But stay within sight."

Ethan nodded and the two ran toward the trees.

"You're good with them," Monica said softly.

"They're good kids." Cash kicked at the ground. His brother had done a fine job with his boys.

Cole had done well with his life, too—building a successful business along with a family. He'd been there for their mom, as well, by opening up his home to her. It was more than could be said for Cash. He came home when he could, but that wasn't often. His mom had no one now—only him.

He felt Monica touch his arm, and tensed. Looking into her eyes, he waited for her to say something, anything beyond the searching look of sympathy she gave him. He backed away. "So what's with this coloring thing you want to do later?"

She dropped her hand. "Well, it's something I read about online last night, while looking up information on how kids grieve."

"Go on." Cash kept his eyes on the boys. Now they were picking flowers amid the tall grass.

"Coloring can be a way of expressing that grief. Maybe it will help unlock Owen's tongue if we share pictures we've made."

"We?" Cash didn't like the sound of that.

"All of us. They follow your lead, Cash. If you open up, they will, too."

Nope. He didn't like the sound of that one bit, but he had to own that he was impressed with her knowledge. She'd looked up this stuff online, which was more than he'd done. He believed in the practical approach, of distracting the kid with new surroundings and fun until he talked.

She touched his arm again. "You need to take time to grieve, too."

Again, he backed away. "This week isn't about what I need. It's about the boys. I owe it to Cole to do what I can, and I can't let death win by keeping Owen's voice silent."

Monica's gaze narrowed. "Win? Life and death isn't a game."

In some ways it was. At least to him. Strategies and planning for missions resembled a game at times. Civilian life was where losses took a vicious bite out of him. They weren't supposed to happen. He'd lost his dad and now his brother. Two of the three men who'd mattered most in his life.

When he didn't answer, Monica's tone softened. "So then you'll color?"

He blew out his breath. It was worth a shot. "Yes, I'll color."

She smiled broadly. But not at him. Her gaze was focused beyond him on the boys, who came running toward her with a handpicked bouquet of a few golden daisy-like flowers with dark centers.

"I love black-eyed Susans. Thank you, guys," Monica gushed.

Owen grinned and Ethan looked pretty proud, too.

Cash chuckled and then clapped his hands together. "Let's load up."

The boys scrambled toward the side-by-sides.

Monica stuck the flowers in her water bottle and set the makeshift vase in the UTV's cup holder.

Cash helped Ethan get settled in while Monica buckled Owen into the bump seat.

"Ready?" he finally asked.

She gave him a thumbs-up.

Starting the engine, Cash waited until Monica started hers and then he gunned it, causing the tires to dig deep and spray dirt and grass her way.

Peering into the side mirror, he spotted her shaking her head.

He might be a lost cause when it came to pushing limits, but tonight he'd try to unlock a couple of his emotional compartments and color for the sake of his nephews. He wasn't making any promises, though.

He'd spent years perfecting the art of keeping his feelings firmly under control. Opening those doors now might do more harm than good. For this mission of helping his brother's boys, he'd do what he could to lead them down the path of expressing their loss. It didn't mean he'd have to fully express his.

Chapter Five

Following Cash, Monica couldn't get his comment out of her thoughts.

I can't let death win.

At first she'd taken it as if life and death were a game, but that didn't quite fit. Cash was a soldier. He knew the cost of death and dying. It was more like he'd personified death into something he could take on and beat. It was as if he personally struggled against it with something to prove. As a marine, how often had Cash faced death? Yet he acted as if he could win by sheer determination. Was that why he lived on the edge? Did he hope to cheat death by pushing himself close to it? What if death finally beat him?

Her stomach clenched at the thought like it always did when she pictured him in combat. Monica hated the idea of him charging into harm's way nearly as much as she respected him for it.

She saw that Cash had pulled into a parking lot filled with other off-road vehicles, effectively interrupting her dark thoughts. There was a mini gas station attached to the restaurant. This place he'd mentioned was not only open for lunch, but looked busy. Really busy.

Cash unbuckled, got out and stretched. "Might be in for a bit of a wait."

"We don't have anywhere we need to be." Monica shrugged, still tangled in those thoughts. What if Cash died in combat— Stop! She wasn't going to think like that. Not today. Not ever.

She slipped off her goggles.

He grinned and reached out to run his index finger down her cheek. "You look like a raccoon with all that dirt on your face except around the eyes."

Monica pulled her head back. "You're not much better."

"You don't have to be so sore about it." Cash gave her a concerned look.

She forced a smile. She hadn't meant to snap at him. Part of her was mad at him for doing what he did, leaving for duty maybe to never return. "I'm not."

"Come on, let's get a table." Cash steered both boys toward the entrance of the restaurant.

Once inside with their names given for the next available table, Monica excused herself. "I'm hitting the bathroom."

"We'll go after you, so we don't lose our place." Cash kept a hand on a shoulder of each of the boys.

"I won't be long." Monica noticed that all three of them had dirty faces, too, so it shouldn't bother her that Cash had pointed out hers. But it did.

In the ladies' room, she quickly washed her face as well as her hands. Running her tinted gloss over her lips, Monica looked hard in the mirror. Was there any point in trying to look good? Once the effects of chemo set in she'd look horrible, more like a plucked stork.

She closed her eyes and took a deep breath. This fear was getting old fast. She'd always obsessed over her appearance but knowing she'd soon look really awful took it to a new level. Growing up with two perfectly sized and beautiful sisters, Monica had never felt comfortable in her own skin. Those insecurities grew worse around Cash. Maybe because she was taller than him, but that wasn't quite it either. Deep down, she'd always wanted him to want a relationship with her but he didn't and never had. She needed to get over it.

Easier said than done. She pinched her cheeks to force some needed color into her face, squared her shoulders and walked out of the restroom. She looked around and spotted Cash waving.

He and the boys were seated in a booth.

She slipped in next to Owen and grabbed a menu. "Anything look good?"

"You did before you washed all that dirt off your face. There's something fetching about a woman who's not afraid to get dirty." Cash gave her a wink.

"What are you talking about?" Monica wasn't in the mood for his teasing.

"Can't you rough it for even a little bit?"

"So I like a clean face. In fact, it'd be a good idea for you to take the boys to wash up before we eat."

"After we order." Cash set his menu down and grabbed her hand, running his fingertip over her manicured nails. "What's with the primping? You didn't used to do all this."

Startled at the zing that scurried up her arm, Monica pulled her hand back. "Some people grow up."

"And some people get caught up in all sorts of images that keep them from being who they are."

"My business is about projecting the right image, so I have to look professional. How is that such a bad thing?"

He paused, as if trying to choose his words carefully. "It's not—"

"Who am I supposed to be, then?" Monica cut him off, but really wanted to know. She was a sister, a daughter, a business owner and now a cancer patient. Who did Cash think she should be?

He appeared cornered, yet his gaze was steady with conviction. "You're meant to be you and you don't have to live up to anyone's idea of perfection. I think you're perfect as you are."

That was not exactly a clear answer and yet it pierced her soul with warmth. She'd never thought she was pretty enough, always too tall and with too big of a nose. Being awkward as a teen with a mouth full of braces hadn't helped how she saw herself either. What was she trying to prove and to whom? And why'd he have to see through to that lack of confidence she still carried deep inside?

The boys were watching them with wide eyes, so Monica changed the subject. "Do you two know what you want for lunch?"

"Pizza," Ethan said.

Monica turned to face Owen. "Is that what you want, too?"

He nodded.

She quickly scanned the menu as the waitress bore down on their table.

"The boys will split a small cheese pizza with ranch dressing on the side. I'll have a deluxe cheeseburger with french fries, and we'll also have three Cokes," Cash ordered.

Monica flashed him a frantic look. She had no idea what she wanted and ended up ordering a chef salad.

"You sure you don't want something more substantial than rabbit food?" Cash teased after the waitress left.

"I happen to like salads. And you pretty much ordered the same thing you ate last night, yet you don't hear me giving you grief." She sat straighter. It wasn't a diet thing, although she wondered if that's what he might be thinking.

What was with him, anyway?

"You just did." He chuckled and then grew serious. "You look good, Monica."

She appreciated the brief flush of pleasure at the compliment until his seriousness turned into a grim scowl. "Now what?"

He shrugged and stood. "Nothing. I'm going to take the boys to wash up."

Monica watched them leave. It was cute how Cash corralled the boys toward the men's room, guiding them. Protecting them. What wasn't cute was that his opinion of her meant way too much and always had.

She cringed as she recalled the first time she'd worn makeup around him. She'd been seventeen and he'd been home on leave. She wanted to make him see her as a real girl, not just her brother's little sister.

She'd gotten a rise out of him alright—but not the grown-up reaction she'd hoped for. His surprise had turned to discomfort when her brother Matthew had teased her about having paint all over her face. She'd been mortified and Cash knew it. He had awkwardly patted her shoulder, telling her she was perfect the way she was.

Just like today with washing off the dirt. No matter what she did in an attempt to charm Cash Miller, it always seemed to backfire on her. Probably a good thing, too.

Cash hurried the boys back to the table. Casting a long look at Monica, he noticed something dark in her eyes as she traced a groove in the wooden tabletop with her finger. Something was definitely going on with her.

Was it that breakup she'd mentioned? Maybe it had been more serious than she'd let on. Cash's gut clenched. He'd like to give that guy a few choice words, perhaps starting with his fist.

It suddenly hit him that maybe he'd caused that look of sadness. Surely his teasing, or his comments about her painted nails, hadn't bothered her. He'd meant it when he said she looked good. Problem was that she looked too good. Still, the Monica he remembered had always given as good or better jabs than any he'd thrown her way.

Just then she caught his gaze and smiled.

It was like hitting a brick wall at full speed, taking away his breath and weakening his knees. Not to mention how his stomach swayed and flipped over. Why had he begged her to stay?

Owen scooted into the booth next to her.

Owen was the reason. His youngest nephew had connected with her and Cash needed to keep that in mind. This weekend wasn't about him. It was about his nephews, about getting Owen to talk, and Monica might be the key to unlocking the kid's vocal chords.

He slipped in next to Ethan. "So tell me about this business of yours."

"I started out with simply a website design service,

but then it morphed into consultative marketing and business branding." Monica sipped her water.

"Branding?" Searing the back end of cattle came to mind.

Monica nodded. "It's a company's promise to their customer. It reinstates what they are and what they want to be, via a slogan or image."

"Is it just you?"

Monica shook her head. "I have an assistant who takes care of the office stuff, like billing and reconciliation of accounts."

He grinned. "Successful?"

She raised one perfectly shaped eyebrow. "I do okay."

Her brother had once told him that she did pretty well. Monica had indeed grown up. To start her own business and actually make it work spoke to her resolve. Making it successful reflected her strength and determination.

She'd never been a quitter. Like a dog on the scent of a buried bone, Monica never gave up when she put her mind to something. Another reason he coveted her help with Owen. He knew she'd give it her all.

He remembered when she'd wanted to play varsity basketball. She hadn't even finished eighth grade when she'd sought his help with her foul shot. They'd practiced for hours through the summer months, and come fall, she was the only ninth grader to make the varsity team.

The waitress arrived with their drinks. Monica had ordered an iced tea instead of pop. Dropping four straws on the table, the waitress said, "Your food will be out soon."

Ethan snatched his straw and blew the paper at his brother.

Owen giggled and did the same back.

Cash dipped his straw wrapper in water, then rolled it between his fingers. He caught Monica's critical gaze.

"You really shouldn't."

He grinned. "They'll learn it in school, anyway."

She tipped her head. "Schools have changed. They come down more on this kind of stuff than when we were kids."

"What are you doing, Uncle Cash?" Ethan zeroed in on him.

"Nothing." Cash crumpled the perfectly made spit-ball into the paper strap that bundled the napkin around the silverware.

The last thing his sister-in-law needed was her boys getting into trouble at school. Cole might have egged him on, but his brother wasn't here. He'd never be here again. Cole had left a huge hole in the world and the reality of that turned Cash's belly sour.

He looked at Monica.

She gave him an encouraging smile as if she could read his thoughts. As if she understood why he'd put away the spitball.

It was an odd sensation, this link with her. This understanding without words.

Just then the food came and Ethan forgot all about straw wrappers and spitballs. Cash watched as Monica helped Owen unravel his napkin. She showed the five-year-old how to place it on his lap, and Cash was struck by how much like a family they were.

This was what he'd steered clear of since becoming a marine. That sourness in his gut strengthened as he considered what he'd missed. What he'd given up. Had he made the right choice?

* * *

By the time they'd finished eating, Cash had paid the bill before Monica could even offer. "Thanks for lunch."

He nodded. "Thanks for staying so we could do this."

"It's been fun." She meant that, too, glad she'd stayed. Glad her thoughts had been diverted from her diagnosis if only for a while.

The boys were anxious to get back on the side-by-sides, but Monica couldn't leave the restaurant just yet. "Sorry, guys, but I need to use the ladies' room."

"Oh no. Can't we go now?" Ethan tipped his head back, clearly frustrated.

Monica ruffled the boy's hair. "I won't be long, I promise."

Ethan didn't look like he believed her.

"Take your time." Cash smiled as he corralled the boys toward the door. "Come on, guys, let's gas up the machines and get in our gear while we wait."

Monica hurried. With no *primping* other than washing her hands, she made it back outside in time to help Owen fasten his helmet strap.

"That was fast." Cash gave her a cheeky grin as he stuffed the gas receipt into his wallet before tucking it in his back pocket.

"I told you I would be." Monica finished with the strap.

"Can we go through another creek?" Ethan's helmet slipped to one side.

Cash knelt down to tighten the strap under the boy's chin. "If we find one."

"Yes-s-s!" Ethan jumped up and down, helmet secure. Owen copied his brother's every move.

"Come on, Owen. Climb up here." Monica patted the bumper seat and then buckled him in.

"Let's take the long way back. There's a trail that heads north toward Munising. We can cut over to Miner's Falls before heading back to your uncle's cabin."

"Sounds good." Monica secured her goggles, slipped behind the wheel, buckled up and started the engine.

Cash peeled out of the restaurant parking lot with a crunch of gravel.

Monica shook her head and followed at a more sedate pace.

It wasn't long before they reached a hilly stretch of trail that followed the power lines. A swath of mounds and dips in the earth stretched before her. Monica remembered coming here once on a snowmobile, and it had been a natural roller coaster ride with all the ups and downs.

Ahead, Cash accelerated.

Monica could hear Ethan's squeals of laughter as they took those dips at midspeed. She glanced at Owen, whose eyes were wide.

"Are you ready for this?"

He nodded.

"Grab my arm if you want me to slow down or stop, okay?" Monica hoped his lunch would stay put. She hoped he might talk, too.

He nodded again, and rocked in the bumper seat as if *telling* her to go.

Monica's heart pinched. If this little guy wouldn't talk during a fun ride, what made her think he'd talk after coloring? What if his issues were deeply psychological?

Just then he gave her a pointed look, communicating very well with those big gray eyes. He wanted to get moving.

"Okay, Owen. Here we go." Monica pressed the gas and off they went along the trail.

The first dip between hills made her belly feel like it floated near her throat, only to fall to her feet as they crested the next hill.

Owen giggled and kicked his feet.

She spotted Cash and Ethan ahead of them, roaring over the last couple of mounds. Encouraged by Owen's obvious enjoyment of the ride, Monica sailed over the hills and tiny valleys, repeating the sensation of floating.

One more mound and dip and they finally pulled over next to Cash and Ethan.

"What'd ya think, Owen? Was that cool or what?" Ethan hollered.

Owen glanced at her.

Monica took a leap of faith. "Go ahead and tell him."

The boy shook his head and then poked at her shoulder. He wanted her to speak for him.

She could easily do that. During their ride, she'd glanced at his smiling face and heard his giggles, but answering for him would only give the kid a pass. Owen needed to talk, and she wasn't going to make it any easier on him to remain quiet.

Hoping she was doing the right thing, Monica shook her head in response. "Oh no. I'm not talking for you. That's your job."

Owen stared her down, but still didn't say a word.

She gave his hand a pat, defeated. "Keep trying."

Cash pulled his side-by-side close. "We need to head home."

Monica tipped her head. "Why, what is it?"

"There's a storm coming in."

She looked up at the sky. There were some clouds, but the sun still blazed, roasting the day. "You're kidding, right?"

"No, I'm not. I received a weather alert on my phone for the area."

Monica sighed. So much for a side trip to the falls. That was too far out of the way. "Alrighty, we'll follow you."

He dipped his head and sped off.

She followed. Glancing at Owen, she took in the child's frown. "Don't worry, Owen. We'll make it back to the cabin."

The boy nodded.

Monica had to hand it to Cash. He certainly was prepared. He'd packed a cooler, as well as a first aid kit, plus he had GPS trail maps and weather alert apps on his phone. He was a marine, so she shouldn't expect anything less.

When they hit a straightaway in the trail, he sped up. Monica followed suit, thinking they'd be home in no time at this pace. But after half an hour of them speeding through the woods, the trail turned twisty and they had to slow to a crawl. It seemed like forever before the trees finally opened up to a broad expanse of meadow.

Monica caught sight of the southwestern sky where dark clouds billowed along the horizon. The temperature had dropped some and the wind had kicked up. They kept up a good speed, but could they outrun the incoming storm?

By the time they were within an hour of the cabin, thunder rumbled in the distance and the wind really whipped. She spotted a small branch in the trail up ahead and hoped Cash saw it, too.

He did. He slowed down and drove over it with a bump.

Monica did the same, glad to hear the giggle out of Owen as they bounced over the obstacle.

The weather moved in fast. The sunshine was gone and the sky darkened. It looked like evening outside instead of late afternoon. They beat the rain, though, pulling onto the driveway leading to her uncle's cabin just as thunder rumbled louder and closer. A brilliant flash of lightning nearly made her jump out of her skin. The horrendous clap of thunder that followed made her teeth rattle.

Owen covered his ears and looked like he might cry.

Monica gave the boy a reassuring pat as she followed Cash into the pole barn and cut the engine. Leaving the keys in place, she pulled off her goggles and helped Owen get unbuckled. They needed to get into the cabin fast. The pole barn was made of metal and she didn't want to be inside it any longer than necessary.

Placing Owen's helmet on the seat, Monica grabbed the boy's hand, ready to run.

"Whoa, slow down. It's okay, we made it," Cash told her.

"I want out of this metal building," Monica said.

He grinned. "The barn is grounded, Monica. It has to be in order to have electric wiring."

"Oh." She'd overreacted again. "Still, I'd rather get the boys inside."

"Agreed." Cash looked at Ethan. "Follow Monica while I put everything away and shut the door."

She grabbed both boys' hands and they ran for the

cabin. Wind roared around them, blowing leaves off trees and stirring up sand from around the firepit into a mini tornado.

After slipping inside through the sliding glass door, she finally exhaled. "Phew, that was close."

"It was cool," Ethan said.

Owen didn't look like he thought so. His bottom lip seemed a little shaky.

They watched as Cash closed the large barn door, secured it and ran for the cabin as huge drops of rain darkened his T-shirt. Then it poured.

Lightning flashed and thunder boomed, shaking the whole cabin. Owen leaned into her.

"Wow. Look at the trees." Ethan stared out the slider.

The trees bent under the torrent of wind as if they were waves rolling in the same direction. Waves that could break.

"Maybe we should get away from the door," Monica suggested. It was glass, and if anything came flying at them, it wouldn't be good.

They backed away just as Cash entered.

"You forgot these." He handed her the water bottle with the black-eyed Susans the boys had picked for her.

She reached for them. "Thanks."

He was soaked, with his hair plastered against his head. "It's crazy out there. Good thing we got home when we did."

"Good thing you're a marine who's prepared. You saved our skin," Monica said.

Cash looked at her, surprised by the fervor in her compliment.

"I mean it. Thank you." Monica smiled.

"You're welcome." He nodded and pulled at the wet T-shirt, which stuck to him like a second skin.

His movements revealed a horrific scar from a gash just above the waistband of his jeans. Monica felt her mouth drop as the blood rushed from her head, making her woozy. She gripped the bottle so hard that water shot up over the top and landed with a splat on the floor.

Cash flushed and gestured toward his room. "I'll change."

"Yeah, do that." She watched his broad back retreat down the hall before she could finally breathe.

Quickly, she set the flowers on the island and grabbed a paper towel to wipe up the spill. She couldn't erase the image of that newly hewn scar still red and puckered from not-too-long-ago stitches from her mind. Like a ragged-edged ribbon, the scar ran across his midsection.

When had he been injured and how?

Monica didn't want to know, but then again maybe she did. One thing she knew for sure—caring for Cash meant a heap of worry and possible loss. It meant facing more scars or worse. She had enough on her plate right now, and falling for Cash Miller was the last thing she needed to do.

For both their sakes, she wouldn't let that happen.

Chapter Six

Cash changed into dry clothes and kicked himself for not teasing Monica when he'd had the chance to divert her attention from his scar. He'd been stunned into silence at the alarm in her eyes. That look of dismay was burned into his memory.

In the past, he'd purposefully kept it light when talking about his soldiering, about his entire career. His scar had brought the danger of what he did front and center without a single word. The reality of being in harm's way had been etched across his belly like a billboard.

Taking a deep breath, he stepped into the kitchen, where Monica was serving milk and cookies to the boys.

"Want some?" she offered, without turning around.

"No, thanks." He slipped by her to grab a glass from the cupboard. After filling it with tap water, Cash downed it in one long gulp, then refilled it.

She wouldn't look at him, but he could feel the tension in her. The curiosity she had over the scar she'd seen. He hoped she wouldn't ask, because it was a story he didn't ever want to tell her.

Combat got super real when it was up close and personal. His experience with face-to-face warfare wasn't something he liked to talk about. Having recently come close to being disemboweled, he'd rather not relive the moment by telling tales. It was bad enough that he sometimes had sensory flashbacks of the spicy breath belonging to the guy who'd managed to slice him under his tactical vest.

More lightning flashed, brightening the cabin, followed by a deep rumble of thunder. He glanced outside. Heavy rain ran down the wall of windows, but through the blur he could see the trees straining under the wind. "It's still coming down pretty hard."

"Yup, and the satellite is out," Monica said.

"We can't watch TV?" Ethan sat in a stool on the other side of the island next to his brother.

"Nope, sorry." Monica bit into a cookie.

"Then it's a good time to color." Cash looked around. "Where are the crayons?"

Monica finally looked at him, her sudden smile brighter than the lightning. "That's right, we were going to draw some pictures. I'll get the stuff."

"Do we have to?" Ethan moaned.

Cash didn't feel like doing it, either, but they'd made a promise to Monica so she'd stay. A promise was a promise and he'd do just about anything for another of her smiles. "Not much else to do right now."

Monica's gaze shifted, sharp as a dagger. "We made a deal."

"That's right, we did," he stated. "Ethan, it's very important to stand by one's word. We agreed to do this so Monica would go riding the UTVs with us, remember?"

Ethan squinted, then nodded.

Owen looked eager to get started. Maybe five-year-olds liked to color.

Monica gathered up crayons, colored pencils and a thick pad of white drawing paper from the hall closet. She spread everything out on the kitchen table. "Sorry, no markers."

Owen climbed into a chair and reached for paper and some crayons. He didn't need any coaxing.

Monica cast him a hopeful glance.

Cash wondered if they shouldn't direct the tyke on what to color, but didn't say anything. This was Monica's show. She was the one who'd read about this exercise in grief therapy online.

Monica slipped into the chair next to his youngest nephew and watched him draw. "Very nice, Owen. That flower looks like the ones you and Ethan gave me today."

So she wasn't giving any instructions. It was all free-form and willy-nilly. Cash stared at his own blank white page. He didn't know how to draw, let alone color. He might as well get the conversation going. "I have no idea how to start."

Ethan had joined them at the kitchen table and waited, too, looking hesitant as if this was some sort of school assignment.

Monica spoke slowly. "We can start with what we did today. Or whatever you're feeling right now. Put that onto paper."

Cash cocked an eyebrow.

She turned back to Owen. "That's pretty."

Cash glanced at the kid's paper. So far, he'd drawn a big yellow flower under a scrawny tree. So much for the release of grief. His picture looked pretty cheerful.

Owen shrugged and reached for a dark blue crayon.

"This is stupid," Ethan huffed.

If Cash didn't get in the game and soon, his oldest

nephew wouldn't take it seriously. It was up to him to get things moving in the right direction. His problem was that there were too many feelings deep down to let them all out on paper, so he started with one thing.

How did he feel right now? He drew a stick figure in the middle of the page. One solitary brown stick figure. His gut clenched and he felt the muscles along his jaw tighten. He was the last man in his family. The only one left.

"Who's that, Uncle Cash?" Ethan looked over his elbow.

"That's me."

"You better draw a gun, too. Dad says soldiers carry guns." Ethan grinned.

Cash glanced at Monica, who was watching wide-eyed. Hearing Ethan reminisce about something Cole might have said had to be a good sign. Ethan had used present tense instead of past, too, as if Cole wasn't gone. And the boy had shared a good memory about his dad. A positive one. That showed some healing was taking place.

Could this thing really work?

The wind whistled outside and rain slammed against the cabin, but inside felt still. Almost too still. Cash cleared his throat. "Maybe we should draw for your dad."

Ethan's face scrunched up as if he couldn't believe what he was hearing. "He can't see them, Uncle Cash. He's dead."

Another punch to the gut.

Owen set his crayon down and stared, his bottom lip trembling.

Now Cash had done it. Messed up good.

"Oh, I'm not so sure that he can't see them."

Monica's soft voice saved the day. "Why don't we color how that makes us feel? Right now, what are you feeling?"

Cash took a deep breath and opened up. "I feel alone."

Ethan looked at him hard. "You got us, Uncle Cash."

Cash thought his heart might break. "Thanks, bud."

Owen had drawn hearts hanging from the scrawny tree branches. Blue hearts with drops of water falling from them.

Cash swallowed hard. The poor kid was crying inside.

Monica saw it, too, and her eyes filled with tears. Not one fell, though. She managed to keep control.

"What about you, Monica? Aren't you going to color, too?" Ethan challenged. He still hadn't made a mark on his own sheet of paper.

Monica didn't bat an eyelash. Instead, she nodded. "I will if you will."

Ethan scowled.

She'd called his bluff.

"I guess we're all coloring now." Cash grabbed a couple more crayons and nodded toward Ethan, who had finally picked up a red pencil. Maybe they'd all learn something through this little exercise.

He didn't care much for what he'd learned so far, because this had brought up concerns he preferred to bury. He was the last man in his immediate family and the only one his mother had left. If he got himself killed, what would that do to her?

He faced five years before he could retire. He'd be no good to anyone without that pension, but what then? He'd always been a marine and there was nothing else he'd rather do.

Staring at his sheet of paper, he silently asked God

for direction knowing he shouldn't expect a clear road map. Maybe the answer was simply trusting God to keep him alive. A challenge, considering the Lord hadn't been there for his brother when that tree fell. God had let Cole die, leaving his boys fatherless and leaving Cash without a brother.

One more person he loved had been taken too soon.

Monica was caught in her own trap. Of course they'd expect her to draw, as well. Holding a crayon poised over her paper, she considered her feelings. A mass of emotions jumbled up inside her—anger, fear, impatience, the desire to trust God completely yet failing.

She pictured the rubber band balls she used to make while working at an office supply store when she was in college. All the different-colored rubber bands wrapped around each other were the crazy thoughts and feelings she'd experienced since having that biopsy that had led to a cancer diagnosis.

Monica started coloring that big ball of rubber bands.

Silence settled over the kitchen table save for the soft scratching of Ethan's colored pencils and the rain hammering the ground outside. The worst of the storm had passed.

Monica had closed most of the windows when they'd arrived except for the one over the sink. Cool, damp air drifted in, confirming that the temperature had plummeted. She shivered.

Cash noticed. "Cold?"

"I'll just close that window." Monica did so quickly and returned to the table.

"I can start a fire," he offered.

"Later. After we color." She didn't want to break out

of this now that Ethan was finally engaged. Peeking at his paper, she wasn't too sure about the fire truck he was drawing with a red pencil. What did that mean?

Glancing at Cash, she noticed that he'd given up drawing and was simply coloring. Blues and greens and purples surrounded his lonely stick figure. Hearing him state that he felt alone had stabbed her quick and hard. The urge to comfort him caught like a thorn in her skin.

She'd encouraged Cash to share and he had, to a degree. Monica knew there was far more to the colors he chose to use. Looking at her own blob, the rubber band ball, she nearly chuckled. She was as bad as he was, playing it safe with her picture. Grazing the surface of feelings instead of digging down deep.

Leaning over Ethan's arm, Monica encouraged the boy. "Nice picture, Ethan. What does it mean?"

The eight-year-old gave her a curious look. "My dad liked fire trucks. You said to draw a picture for him."

"Yes, I did." Monica silently scolded herself as a fool. Some things were simply what they were, and yet she tried to read more into them. She didn't know what she was doing, trying to play therapist.

The article she'd read had made it sound so easy, and yet here they were, drawing and coloring, and no one was unloading what lay heavy in their hearts. Even if they had, she didn't have the training to know how to respond properly.

Only Owen's picture clearly depicted his sorrow, and he still wasn't saying a word.

Chewing her bottom lip, she peeked again at his paper. He'd drawn a cheerful little house with smoke plumes coming from a chimney. "Is that your house, Owen?"

He shrugged.

Ethan included a dog near the fire truck, one with spots.

"Do you guys have a dog?" Monica asked.

"No." Ethan's face fell. "Mom's allergic to dogs."

Like she was allergic to pine. Monica's heart pinched. What was their mother like? And how was she taking the death of her husband, leaving her boys without their dad? Worrying about losing her hair seared Monica's conscience. There were far worse things to lose.

She cleared her throat. "I'm sorry."

Ethan looked at her funny. "For what?"

"That you can't have a dog." She heard the quaver in her voice.

Evidently Cash did, too, and he reached for her hand, giving her fingers a soft squeeze.

Monica nearly lost it then, but didn't. She clung to him, wishing she could make things all better for everyone.

"What's that?" Ethan looked at her picture.

She pulled her hand away from Cash. "It's a rubber band ball."

Again Ethan gave her an odd look. "Why'd you draw that?"

Why, indeed? Maybe she should be the one who shared a little. "Sometimes my feelings get all jumbled up like a big ball of…"

"Rubber bands?" Cash raised an eyebrow.

Monica met his concerned gaze and nodded.

He stared at her as if trying to unravel those rubber bands one by one.

As if he could. Some of those bands resulted from

him, too. She looked away, concentrating on Ethan's picture as the boy set down a brown pencil. "Done?"

"Yeah." He leaned back in his chair.

"Could you draw another one?"

Owen nodded and grabbed a fresh piece of paper. He still didn't speak.

Ethan shrugged and tore a new sheet from the pad in turn.

Monica looked at the clock. It was nearly five thirty. A good time to start dinner. There was still ground beef in the fridge, but it was too wet outside to grill. "I'm going to make dinner while you guys keep coloring. Do you like spaghetti?"

"Yeah!" Ethan smiled.

Owen did, too.

Cash didn't. He looked at her as if she'd just chickened out. "Want some help?"

"I got this." She stood and patted his shoulder. "You keep drawing with your nephews."

Monica hoped they might open up some more, but probably not. This exercise hadn't resolved anything. Owen remained as tight-lipped as before. There had to be something to get the boy to speak, but what?

Cash stared at his lone stick figure surrounded by dark colors. Dark green, dark blue, dark purple, burgundy and even charcoal-gray. He didn't use black—that seemed too cliché, and his feelings weren't quite that horrific. He realized that anger could be expressed in a myriad of dark colors. It was sort of freeing, too, all those variations.

He pulled off a new piece of paper and scribbled some more. No more stick figures, just color. Confusion seemed to be the theme of this portrait. The new hues were lighter, softer even, in shades of gray and tan that bled into almond. The box had a crayon color named almond, go figure.

The scent of frying beef mixed with onions, garlic and oregano teased, and confusion morphed into hunger. He glanced at Monica's rendering of a rubber band ball. Her feelings were jumbled, she'd said. When it came to her, his were, too. A mass of contradictions.

He grabbed a bright blue crayon that reminded him of Monica's eyes, one called cerulean. He filled in the middle of the page. Hunger transformed into a longing so sharp that it pierced deep. More shades of blue came out of the box of crayons, because sometimes her eyes looked almost turquoise in the right light.

His fingers grabbed a red crayon and he suddenly scoured through the other colors in frustration. He sat back, halting this "feelings on parade" exercise.

Cash didn't want to feel. He'd practiced compartmentalizing his emotions for years and in one exercise of putting crayons to paper, he'd let loose the Pandora's box of his heart. He mentally shut the lid. Tight.

He glanced at the subject of his frustration. Monica was opening canned tomatoes and dumping the contents into a steaming pot. She added more spices and then grabbed a spoon in order to taste the sauce. She sprinkled in a bit of sugar and stirred. He'd never gone to that kind of trouble for spaghetti sauce. He simply opened up a jar from the store and called it good.

He checked on the boys. They were still scribbling pictures. Owen drew birds and sunshine and clouds, while Ethan tried to draw Dogman.

Cash smiled as he got up and headed toward Monica.

Her back was to him, so he drew close and peeked over her shoulder. "Smells good."

She jumped slightly, landed against his chest, then jerked away. "You shouldn't sneak up on people."

He noticed that she sucked at her thumb. "What happened?"

She glared at him. "I burned it when you stalked up behind me."

He laughed out loud and took a step toward her. "I didn't stalk."

"Oh, I think you did." She stepped back.

He reached for her hand. "Let me see."

"No need."

"Come on, Stork. Give me your hand." Cash took hold of her slender fingers and inspected the burned thumb. A small welt had already formed under the skin.

He hit the automatic ice dispenser on the fridge and grabbed a small handful of cubed ice. After tossing all but one in the sink, he rubbed that last piece along the welt.

Glancing at her face, he noticed that her eyes were closed, but not with pleasure. Her jaw was clenched as if she was trying to get control of those rubber band emotions.

She opened her eyes and stared straight at him, and she looked mad.

"What's wrong?" he whispered.

"Nothing. Just stop, okay?" Monica pulled her hand away.

"Stop what?" He spread his arms as if innocent, but he knew. She didn't want this pull between them any more than he did. And yet he pushed it. Pushed *her* when he knew better.

Just then Owen squealed, as Ethan held his colored pencil drawing of Dogman up to his face and growled.

Cash rolled his eyes. "Ethan!"

Owen screamed and ran for the bedroom, with his brother in hot pursuit.

Cash charged toward the room the boys shared. Owen had thrown himself on the bottom bunk, his shoulders shaking. The tyke was crying. "Come on, Ethan. You know better."

Ethan looked indignant. "I was only teasing."

"Yeah, well, stop teasing." Cash reached for Owen. "Come on, buddy, it's not that big a deal. It's just a drawing."

Owen remained facedown, but his sobs were softer now.

Cash rubbed the kid's back. Glancing at Ethan, he noted that the older boy looked contrite. "Go help Monica set the table."

Ethan drooped his shoulders, but did as he was told without a word.

Everyone seemed touchy after the coloring exercise. Maybe some good would come from it. Cash tried again. "Owen, come on, buddy, enough with the tears. Tell me what's up."

Owen shook his head.

"Still not talking."

Another head shake. He wasn't crying, though.

"Can you sit up?" Cash coaxed.

The boy did so, rubbing his eyes.

"I know this isn't easy, Owen. I miss your dad, too."

Owen's eyes widened.

"If you need to cry, I suppose that's okay." Cash didn't believe his own words. Crying didn't change a thing.

Owen rested his hand on Cash's arm.

"What?"

Owen gave him a pointed look.

If the kid could write full sentences, Cash would have given him pen and paper. What was he trying to say?

The boy reached up and touched Cash's face, then his eye, and drew a finger down Cash's cheek.

Cash finally got it. "Do I cry?"

Owen nodded.

He thought about the question before answering. If he said he never did, that would negate what he'd just told the boy. Owen was only five, far too young to stuff his feelings down deep where they'd stay put. He didn't want to patronize the boy, either, by telling him that he'd cried a lot at Owen's age.

The truth was that after Cash's own father had died, he'd sworn he'd never cry again. He'd broken that vow when his commanding officer, riddled with bullet holes, lay gasping his last breath. Crying did no good. It didn't bring anyone back.

Looking at his youngest nephew, Cash decided on honesty. "I feel like crying a lot sometimes."

Owen chewed on that for a bit, took a deep breath and stood, dry-eyed. The boy was bucking up. Then he grabbed Cash's hand to lead him back out into the kitchen, where dinner was smelling close to being done.

Cash smiled at the kid. He'd answered truthfully, but incorrectly. He'd just taught his five-year-old nephew to set aside his feelings. Whether that was good or bad, Cash didn't know, but it suddenly made him feel like crying.

Chapter Seven

After dinner, cleanup and a call from the boys' mom, Monica gathered everyone in the living room for a movie. The heavy rain had tapered off to a fine, cold drizzle, allowing the satellite to come back on, but there was nothing worth watching on TV.

Monica looked over the stash of DVDs in the drawer of the entertainment hutch, while Cash built a fire in the woodstove. After running her finger over the spines of a dozen family films, she lifted up a tried-and-true favorite. "How about *Star Wars*?"

Ethan scrunched up his face. "We've seen it."

"Hmm. How about this one?" Monica grabbed a Disney flick.

"Seen that, too."

Monica shared a look with Cash.

"Ethan, help her find a movie."

The boy got up from the couch as if it took every ounce of his energy to do so. He looked over the DVDs with a critical eye, breezing past several animated films to finally settle on an old John Wayne movie. "This one."

Monica chuckled. "Works for me. Popcorn?"

Ethan grinned. "Yes, please."

"I love popcorn." She didn't bother adding that dousing the kernels with melted butter was the reason why she loved it. That much was obvious.

"Me, too," Ethan agreed.

Monica smiled at the boy's politeness and hurried back to the kitchen for the Zelinsky family popcorn pan. Her uncle believed in popping corn on the stove instead of the microwave, and Monica agreed. Heating the oil, she spotted Owen helping Cash.

The five-year-old handed his uncle small logs from the wood bin.

"Thanks, buddy." Cash's voice was deep but gentle.

Monica melted butter in a small saucepan on the next burner before dumping the popcorn into the hot oil. After watching the kernels sizzle until one popped, then another, she placed a lid on the pan and shook it across the burner. More kernels popped and she breathed in the mouthwatering aroma.

When the popping sounds finally stopped, she dumped the contents into a large bowl, followed by the melted butter and salt, and then headed for the living room with a wad of napkins.

Cash was seated in one corner of the large sectional couch. He lifted the remote. "Everyone ready?"

Monica took the other end, while the boys sat between them.

Owen scooted closer to her.

"Ready," Ethan said, around a mouthful of popcorn.

Cash hit Play, then glanced at her. "Thanks for the popcorn."

She smiled, her mouth full, too.

The cabin warmed up quickly with the fire blazing,

and as the movie played on, the boys grew still. Owen, snuggled into the crook of her arm, was soon fast asleep and Ethan's eyelids kept drooping. It wasn't even eight o'clock, but they'd had a big day.

Monica shifted carefully.

Owen startled, then shifted and settled back into slumber.

"We should probably put them to bed," she whispered to Cash, whose eyes looked like they might drift closed any minute now, too.

"Yeah." Cash stood and stretched. "Come on, boys, let's go."

Ethan mumbled something, but got up without complaint and headed for the bathroom.

"Here, I'll take Owen." Cash bent down to lift the boy from her lap.

That placed Cash's face very close to her own. Monica stole a peek at his strong jaw and the muscle that flexed there, as if he'd also noticed how close they were.

"Need help?" she managed to ask, when Cash straightened with Owen in his arms.

"I've got it."

She hit Pause on the remote and also stood. She gathered up the napkins and popcorn bowl, while listening to Cash encourage his nephews to go to the bathroom and wash their hands.

Setting the empty bowl in the sink, she felt her stomach turn soft and squishy at the sound of that deep, gentle voice coaxing the boys like a pro. Cash Miller was a good guy. He'd always been one of the good guys and he'd make a great dad if he ever got around to getting married—

She stopped that train of thought. It was a dead end. She knew better than to consider marriage and Cash

Miller in the same sentence. Dangerous thoughts. Dangerous man.

"Monica, can you come in and pray with us?" Cash called.

Her heart stuck in her throat as if he'd caught her in those thoughts. "Be right there."

Taking a deep breath, Monica entered the boys' room. Ethan was tucked into the top bunk and Owen was on the bottom. The last time she was in here, Ethan had woken from a bad dream. She hoped he slept well tonight. Was that why Cash was praying over them?

Cash reached out his hand to her. "If you'll touch Owen's forehead, I'll cover Ethan's."

Monica nodded and slipped her hand into Cash's. There was no ignoring the butterflies let loose in her belly when he threaded his fingers through hers. Those butterflies sneaked right up her arm, too, causing all kinds of havoc to her senses.

Get a grip already.

Focusing on the task before her, she ruffled Owen's hair, then covered his forehead with her palm. She closed her eyes when Cash started to pray.

"Dear Father in heaven, please watch over these boys as they sleep and give them a good night's rest. Protect them, Lord. Amen." His deep voice rumbled over her. Through her.

"Amen," she said in unison with Ethan.

Owen simply nodded.

Cash slipped his hand to the small of her back and led her toward the door, where he stopped and turned off the light. "Good night, guys."

"Night, Uncle Cash," Ethan responded. "Good night, Monica."

"Good night." Monica noticed that Owen had already drifted back to sleep.

She hurried out before Cash touched her again. Turning toward him, she quickly said, "I might as well turn in, too, so I can get an early start for home in the morning."

"It's way too early. Sit with me."

Monica opened her mouth to refuse, but nothing came out.

"Please?"

Curiosity fought apprehension and won. Cash Miller might be dangerous, yet she followed him right back to the couch.

Cash reached for a bottle of water from the fridge, then offered it to Monica. "Want one?"

She took it, barely meeting his gaze.

He grabbed another and headed to his corner of the couch, stretching out his legs onto the coffee table. "You okay?"

"Yeah, why?" She sat down at the other end.

"I don't know. You seem quiet." He'd never known Monica to be quiet other than when she was angry. As kids, he used to tease her until she got mad and super quiet, then he'd tease her some more until she finally laughed.

He didn't feel like teasing her tonight, though. Something was definitely going on with her and he wanted to know what it was. "Why'd you come up here all alone?"

She shrugged.

He listened to the quiet in the cabin, glad the rain had brought them indoors. Glad the boys had gone to bed early. "Come on, Monica, it's me you're talking to. What's up?"

She gave him a wan smile. "Sometimes the stress of daily life gets to me, so I get away. By myself."

"What's daily life like for you?"

She looked at him then. "My business keeps me busy, between web design and marketing on a consultative basis. I've even got some influential clients I meet with regularly."

He liked the proud tilt to her chin. She'd built a business by herself and he'd guess she did it her way. With her rules. "That guy you were dating. Did he mess you up?"

She laughed. "No."

He gave her a pointed look.

She added simply, "He's a nice enough guy, but sort of spineless now that I think on it. We weren't really serious, so he ducked out of the picture."

"His loss." Cash meant that.

"What about you? Anyone special?" Her gaze darted to her feet before she folded those long legs underneath her.

He recalled the one kiss they'd shared all those years ago, when she'd turned eighteen. The power of it had knocked his socks off and he'd steered clear of repeating it ever since. The memory tempted him, though. Seeing Monica seated close enough to touch tempted him badly, but kissing her a second time might prove even more impactful, and then what?

He couldn't afford falling for her. He was an all-or-nothing kind of guy. He gave his career his all and it demanded that much and more. Men's lives depended on him keeping a clear head and making quick decisions. Worrying about his own safety didn't enter that equation when there was no one waiting back home for him.

The cost of loving a woman, especially this woman, was simply too high.

"Other than you?" He gave her a teasing wink. "Nope."

She looked at him then. "Why?"

Those bright blue eyes of hers pierced deep, forcing him to give an honest answer. "I won't compromise the safety of my men with personal worries."

Monica chuckled. "So a woman is worrisome to you?"

He smiled, too. "In every way imaginable."

She rolled her eyes, but seemed to understand. In fact, she understood him better than most.

"What about you? Why no husband and two point five kids?"

"Haven't met the right man, I guess."

Cash nodded. "He's out there."

She looked away. "Maybe. So, why'd you join the marines, anyway? Neither your dad or Cole were military."

Back to him. She was good at deflecting any digging into her personal life. He probably shouldn't go there anyway, so he thought about her question a moment. "After my dad died, I needed to beat death. I wanted to face it and beat it. I thought joining the marines would give me that opportunity."

She narrowed her gaze. "Did it?"

He thought about all those colors he'd drawn earlier. The anger and frustration… "In some respects, it has, but the older I get the more I'm learning how little control I have over anything. Cole was supposed to live longer than me."

Monica's eyes filled with tears, but she didn't reach out. She simply stared at him and into him, as if she could delve into his soul and soothe it. Soothe him. Good old Monica. What would he do without her?

The scary thought of actually losing her slipped through his mind and nearly choked him. He took a long pull from his bottle of water. Funny, but Monica was one of those stable forces in his life. She'd grown up, she'd dressed up with her sparkly clothes and makeup but she hadn't changed much. Not really. She was still his *Stork*.

"You want to finish watching that movie?" He needed to end this conversation fast before he said something he shouldn't like she'd always be his.

"No." Her voice was whisper soft.

He glanced at her mouth, wanting to taste those lips one more time.

She caught him and blushed.

He stood before he did something they'd both regret. "You're right, Stork. I think I'll turn in early, so I can see you off in the morning."

Monica looked relieved as she got up in turn. She didn't even seem to mind him calling her the hated nickname. "With more pancakes? I brought blueberries."

He cupped her face. "Anything you want. I owe you big time for staying and helping with the boys. Thank you."

Her eyelids closed and she leaned into his hand briefly before stepping back. "No problem. I needed this—" Her voice broke, so she cleared her throat. "Night, Cash."

"Good night." He watched her dart up the stairs to the loft.

Something weighed heavily on her mind and he'd let her go without finding out what. He'd let her down. But then, maybe that was for the best. He'd meant it when he'd told her he needed to keep his mind clear when he returned to his company. The safety of his men and each mission depended on him becoming a machine with only one goal—success.

He usually turned the care of his family over to God when he left the States. Whatever was going on with Monica, Cash prayed God would take care of it. Although God hadn't exactly come through this last time, letting Cole die in a freak accident, Cash prayed anyway. He still believed in a God who was bigger than his anger and frustration.

God knew what He was doing even if Cash didn't agree with the way things turned out. Cash might struggle with answers to many questions, but his concern for Monica demanded that he pray. It was really all he could do.

Early the next morning, Monica looked in the mirror and grimaced at her puffy eyes staring back. She'd had a fitful night of sleep after crying her heart out, her face plastered into a pillow so Cash wouldn't hear. She couldn't believe she'd woken up so early, but then she'd gone to bed pretty early, too.

Last night, she'd nearly blurted out the truth. She'd come so close to telling Cash about the cancer because of the tender look in his eyes. She'd been even closer to snuggling into his strength. The guy was a rock, but he'd lost his father and now his brother. It wouldn't be fair to burden him with her issues.

Hadn't he said the last thing he wanted was a woman back home to worry about? She certainly didn't want Cash distracted while deployed. She wanted him safe and sound. She wanted him alive, and if the truth were told, she wanted him to be hers.

She leaned her head back and nearly cried again. That wasn't ever going to happen. Even if he wanted her, which he didn't, she couldn't do that to him. Not now. Not when her future hung in the balance of cancer treatments. Not when she might not have a whole body in the end. She slammed her pajamas into the suitcase and zipped it closed.

Good thing she was leaving. For both their sakes.

Padding down the steps from the loft as quietly as she could manage, Monica wasn't surprised to see Cash already up and making coffee. The sight of him in a T-shirt and pajama bottoms, with his hair mussed, nearly let loose the waterworks. The sad truth was that she'd fallen for Cash Miller a long time ago and all those feelings were rushing back in on her.

He turned and smiled when he saw her. "Morning, Stork."

"Morning." Her voice didn't sound like her own.

His gaze narrowed. "You look awful. Are you feeling okay?"

"Thanks a lot. You really know what to say to a girl." She didn't bother to hide her irritation.

He looked concerned. "Seriously, your face is all puffy."

She rolled her eyes and thought quickly. "Probably all the salt from the popcorn last night." She held up her hands. "See? Sausage fingers."

He took both her hands in his, gently rubbing her fingers as he looked them over. "They look pretty slender to me."

She pulled her hands back and hurried into the kitchen. "I can finish making the coffee while you work on the pancakes."

His gaze narrowed as he looked at her, but finally he let it go. "Sounds like a plan."

They worked together in silence. Cash tossed some bacon in a hot frying pan before mixing up the pancake batter. She grabbed the container of blueberries and washed them in the sink while inhaling the luscious scent of frying bacon.

She was careful to keep her distance, not even letting her elbow brush his. He seemed to be doing the same thing.

A loose blueberry rolled off the counter and tumbled to a stop next to Cash's bare foot. She bent to pick it up before he stepped on it. Monica had never noticed his feet before. They were nicely shaped and solid, like the rest of him.

Straightening up, she tossed the rogue berry in the trash, then grabbed a mug for coffee. "I waited until it was done brewing."

He nodded as he stirred in the blueberries. "I noticed that."

"Do you want a cup?"

"Please."

She handed him the first serving, then found another mug for herself and added cream and sugar. After fetching the butter and syrup from the fridge, she sat on a stool at the island and watched him pour puddles of batter on the griddle. "I'll leave the food I brought."

"Thanks." He didn't look up from the stove, taking care to turn the strips of bacon over.

"You're pretty comfortable in the kitchen."

"Have to be if I want to eat."

"No mess halls on base? Wait, do you live on base?"

He chuckled. "Yes, I do. I have a pretty nice town house, too."

What would his place look like? She'd been inside the house where Cash grew up only once, after his father had died. She'd felt like the awkward stork she'd been.

She fell silent and sipped her coffee. There were too many memories between them. Too many questions she shouldn't even ask, so she remained quiet while Cash finished cooking their breakfast.

He set a plate with two pancakes stuffed with bleeding blueberries in front of her, followed by a plate with all the bacon. "Help yourself."

She grabbed a strip of bacon and wolfed it down. "Thanks."

He sat next to her with his own plate of pancakes, which he covered with syrup.

Monica couldn't stop noticing things she hadn't paid attention to before, like the small scar on Cash's left wrist. Reaching out, she ran her finger over the white line of skin and felt him tense. "What happened here?"

He smiled as if the memory was a good one. "Snowmobiling with your brothers up here. I got tangled up in some barbed wire that slipped between my jacket sleeve and glove."

She grabbed his hand and turned it over. No scar there. It only ran along the top of his wrist. "Please don't tell me you ran into it while driving the sled."

He chuckled. "No. We were breaking trail and there was a fallen bit of fencing in the way. I grabbed one end while Matthew grabbed the other, and my hand got in the way."

"Stitches?" Monica asked.

Cash shrugged. "Probably should have. That wire cut pretty deep, but no."

Her amusement died when she recalled the broad scar across his belly. That hadn't looked like something he'd received while having fun. That had battle scar written all over it and she didn't want to think about how he'd gotten it.

Sinking deeper into dark thoughts, she considered the kind of scars she might end up with. How visible would they be?

Staring at the butter melting over her pancakes, Monica wasn't so hungry anymore. But she couldn't let these beauties go to waste, especially since she didn't know when she'd enjoy a stack of blueberry pancakes with Cash again. More dark thoughts.

Dousing the stack with syrup, she dug in with a vengeance. "These are really good. Thank you."

"You're welcome."

They polished off the pancakes and bacon, and too soon it was time for Monica to go.

Cash grabbed her suitcase and carried it out the door.

Once outside, they both looked around. Fallen tree branches and leaves littered the grass. The skies were clearing as the sun made a modest appearance in the east, but the grounds were a mess.

"Whoa. Maybe I should stick around and clean up."

He waved her suggestion away. "We got this. It'll give me something to do with the boys. Text me when you get home."

Monica nodded, staring at his bare feet a moment before looking him in the eye. She should give him a hug, but...

"Tell the boys I said goodbye. Tell them I'm sorry I

didn't say it in person, but I have to get home." Before she did something she'd regret, like tell Cash everything, including how she felt about him.

"I will and they'll be fine."

Monica stepped forward and extended her arms. She wanted that hug. "Later, Cash. It was good to see you."

His arms wrapped around her waist and he drew her close, much too close for a quick embrace between friends. He buried his face in her hair and whispered, "Take care, Monica."

She held on a moment longer, savoring the feel of his broad shoulders under her palms. She melted against him when his lips brushed her jaw and the whiskers of his short beard scraped her chin.

She ended the sweet torment by pulling away, fast. "I better go."

"Yeah, you should." He ran his hand over his chin, looking troubled. Dangerous.

She climbed behind the wheel of her car and then glanced up at him, memorizing his face, his eyes and the way he looked at her.

Cash held the door and then shut it, tapping on the roof. "Be safe, Stork."

"You, too." She started the engine and backed up, turned around and headed down the driveway.

Tears blurred her vision.

After last night, she hadn't thought she had any tears left. It was better this way. Once they were out of sight, they'd be out of each other's minds. That was how it worked. How it had always worked.

Remembering the feel of his embrace, she wondered if it might be different this time. What if she couldn't shake her thoughts of Cash? Her feelings.

Turning a corner, Monica groaned when she spotted the fallen tree up ahead. A huge maple lay across the driveway. She slowed to a stop, put the car in Park and got out. The tall, jagged stump showed signs of charring from being hit by lightning.

There was no driving around it either way, due to the density of trees lining the only entrance to her uncle's cabin. This was the only way out, too. She wasn't going anywhere today.

Grabbing her cell phone, she called her mother and explained the situation.

"What about your doctor's appointment this Thursday?" Her mom's voice sounded a little shrill.

Monica knew how she felt. They were mere days away from Thursday. They both wanted to get moving on this cancer thing. Monica needed to agree on a plan, get it started and get it done.

"I'll be home in plenty of time." She hoped. "We just have to get someone out here to remove the tree. I'll keep you posted."

After disconnecting, Monica sighed. It was Sunday. They wouldn't get ahold of anyone today. At best they might leave a message and hear back tomorrow.

For now, she was stuck here. With Cash.

She thought about that embrace once again and shuddered. This wasn't good. Not good at all.

Chapter Eight

Cash spotted Monica's car coming back to the house and frowned. She must have forgotten something. He hoped they didn't have to repeat their goodbye. That embrace was something he didn't think he could repeat. It had nearly killed him not to kiss her.

Stepping out onto the deck, so he didn't wake the boys, he spread his arms. "What'd you forget?"

She got out of the car, a look of panic etched across her face. "I can't get out. There's a tree down, blocking the drive."

His stomach sank. "Can't you drive around it?"

Now she looked irritated. "If I could have, I'd be gone."

He took a deep breath and reentered the house.

She followed him and watched silently as he donned a pair of work boots. Then she followed him back outside. "What are you doing?"

"There's a chain saw in the pole barn. Stay with the boys."

She laughed. "There's no way you can cut through that trunk with the chain saw that's here."

Now he was irritated. "We'll see."

"Cash, I'm serious. It's a huge tree and the trunk is covering the drive, not the branches. You'll hurt yourself."

He gave her a look that said that he'd handle it.

She responded by raising one perfectly arched eyebrow.

Without a word, he exited the cabin for the pole barn. He'd figure it out. It wasn't like he had much of a choice.

Armed with the gas-powered chain saw, which did seem a little puny when he thought about it, Cash walked down the drive. He could feel Monica's gaze burning holes in his back, but he wasn't about to turn around or argue. He'd assess the situation and report back.

It didn't take long to find the tree. Lightning had splintered the huge trunk, but Cash believed it was the wind that had brought the bulky maple down. He looked at the chain saw in his hand and snorted. Even though Monica was probably right, he'd give it a try. Thinking about that embrace only added more resolve. He had to make an attempt.

Taking off the blade cover, he pulled the start cord, adjusted the choke and pulled again. The saw whirred to life.

He stepped forward, kicking himself for wearing his pajamas instead of changing into jeans. If the blade kicked back there was little to protect him.

Monica was right again.

He growled and tipped the blade, cutting into the trunk at an angle. It didn't take him long to realize this wasn't going to work. After the blade got stuck for a second time and stalled, he pulled it free and considered the situation.

He could clear a way around the base of the maple, but tossed that idea aside, as it would involve felling other trees that were too big for the puny chain saw. He'd cut down a couple small trees in his day, but he was by no means an expert. His brother had been, and he'd been killed by a tree that had turned on him.

Cash blew out his breath. Monica was not only right, but she was stuck. Here. With him.

And the boys. Thankfully.

They had plenty of food, and the side-by-sides if an emergency arose. He grabbed his phone from one of his pajama bottom pockets and called his sister-in-law.

"Hi, Cash." She yawned.

Realizing it was still pretty early, he apologized. "Sorry if I woke you."

"No, no. I'm up and just making coffee. Are the boys okay?"

"They're fine and still sleeping. Listen, we got hit pretty hard with the storm that rolled through, and there's a huge maple down, blocking the driveway to the cabin. Can you get some of your guys on it? It's too big for me to cut with the chain saw that's here."

"I'll see what I can do, but it won't be for a few days. Cole's foreman just called to say they've received tons of requests already."

"There's no driving around it, so you'll have to park and walk in a good stretch." Cash expected her along with his mom on Tuesday. Would they still make it?

"Got it. I'll see what I can do and call you when I know more."

"Thanks, Ruth." He pocketed the phone and then sheathed the chain saw blade. Slowly, he made his way back to the Zelinsky cabin. And Monica.

The hug they'd shared burned through him as if he were feeling it all over again. The luscious smell of her hair, the delicate width of her pressed against him... She was tall, sure, but oh so slender.

What was he going to do with her until the driveway was clear?

Nothing. He'd keep his distance like always and hope his brother's tree service crew came quickly.

Monica paced the living room, keeping her eyes fixed on the windows so she could spot Cash when he appeared around the curve in the driveway. She didn't dare call him, which might distract him while using the chain saw. She wasn't even sure he had his phone on him.

It was nearing eight o'clock and the boys still slept. Surely they'd wake up soon. She hoped they would. At least the boys drew the focus away from the two of them.

Finally, she spotted Cash walking toward the house, chain saw in hand and a deep frown pulling down his shapely lips. She knew he couldn't cut through that thick trunk.

He set the chain saw on the deck and stepped inside. "You want the good or bad news first?"

A cold sliver of dread pierced her. "Does it matter?"

He chuckled. "No, I suppose not. The good news is that I called my sister-in-law and she'll send a team from their tree service out to clear away that maple."

Monica scrunched her nose. "And the bad?"

"It might take a few days for them to get here. Their area got hit, too, so they're already knee-deep in cleanup work."

Monica's heart froze. "A few days? I need to be home before Thursday."

His gaze narrowed. "What's going on Thursday?"

"I have a meeting I can't miss." She looked away. How on earth was she going to keep quiet about her cancer diagnosis for the next few days?

"What time?"

"What does that matter?"

"What time is your meeting?" he pressed.

"Afternoon, but still, I don't want to be strolling home that morning. I have to prepare and, well, it's in Petoskey—a good half-hour drive or more even in end-of-summer traffic."

"Ruth misses her boys, so I'm sure she'll get the guys here in time."

Monica nodded, hoping he was right. After taking a deep breath, she blew it back out. She needed something to keep her busy, and physical labor was a good enough cure for being antsy. "Might as well start clearing the grounds around here."

Cash smiled as he took in her sparkly T-shirt and Levi's. "You might want to change into something you can get dirty."

"These are old, so it's fine. Shouldn't you put on some jeans?"

He chuckled. "Yeah, probably should. I'll be right out."

She swung her thumb toward the boys' room. "Should we wake them?"

Cash shook his head. "Let them sleep. They'll find us outside soon enough."

Monica fished in the downstairs closet for a pair of work boots and changed out of her tennis shoes. The boots were roomy, so she grabbed another pair of socks before stepping outside.

Once in the yard, she breathed in the cool morning air. The sun shone from a cloudless blue sky. It was as if yesterday's storm hadn't even happened. Until she looked around.

Branches, leaves and downed limbs littered her uncle's property. A scraggly pine had been blown down, just missing the pole barn. Trudging to the barn, she opened the door and fetched a wheelbarrow, loppers and work gloves. She and Cash had their work cut out for them, but it would keep them busy until the driveway was clear.

She got started picking up the smaller stuff, filling the wheelbarrow a couple times while wondering what was taking Cash so long. She had her answer when he stepped out the sliding glass door with his nephews in tow. Owen munched on a piece of toast.

"Monica, put them to work while I get the chain saw."

"Let's get you boys some work gloves." She waved them over. When they stood before her, she knelt and touched each boy's shoulder. "Listen close. You need to stay away from your uncle while he's using the chain saw."

Owen nodded.

"We know. Our dad taught us what to do. We used to help him gather wood, too, you know." Ethan puffed up his chest.

"Okay, good." Monica's heart twisted as she handed each boy gloves that were a little big.

She'd been here only a couple days, but she loved these two little boys. How quickly they'd sneaked into her heart, and being stuck here would only make it harder to say goodbye. She might not get the chance to duck out like she'd tried this morning. Who knew when or if she'd ever see any of them again? More heavy thoughts to drag her down.

"Alright then, let's tackle this mess." Monica forced a smile, glad the boys didn't complain.

All of them spent a good part of the morning clearing branches. Cash cut the fallen pine into logs that he stacked next to the barn. They would work well in the firepit. The top of the pine he dragged into the tall grass beyond the backyard, but not too close to the woods. Cash had promised the boys that they'd burn the pile when they were done.

Monica stretched and her stomach growled. It wasn't quite time for lunch, but she wanted something. Scooping up their empty water bottles littering the firepit area, she figured they needed a break. "Anyone hungry for a snack?"

"I am!" Ethan raced for the deck.

Owen followed, tripped and fell in the grass, then got back up. No tears and nothing hurt.

Monica looked for Cash, shading her eyes from the bright sunlight. The day was growing warmer by the hour and sweat trickled down her back.

Inside the cabin, the air still felt cool from the night before. She spotted Cash, chain saw in hand, making quick work of another large branch that had fallen from a maple in the front yard. The back of his T-shirt showed a damp line of sweat and his muscles flexed as he worked. The jeans he'd put on had smudges of mud and chain saw grease along his backside. He looked at ease even while working hard.

When he turned off the saw and wiped at his brow, she stepped out onto the front deck and hollered, "Cash, we're taking a break. Are you hungry?"

"I could eat." He gave her a crooked grin that knocked her for a loop.

The butterflies in her belly threatened to overtake the hunger pangs. So sharp was the sensation of longing for a life with Cash that she grabbed her midsection as if to quiet all the rumblings there.

She hurried into the kitchen. Pulling lunch meat and cheese from the fridge, she went about the task of making sandwiches, but looked up when Cash entered the cabin.

He headed straight for the kitchen sink to wash his hands, passing by her. He smelled like the outdoors and sweat and the two-cycle engine fuel mixture from the chain saw.

Monica did her best to ignore the heady scent of him. Ignore his presence behind her at the sink. She handed Ethan and Owen, both seated at the island, paper plates with half a turkey sandwich and potato chips on each. "If you want more, I'll make it."

"Yes, please." Ethan sank his teeth into his sandwich.

"You haven't finished that one yet." Cash leaned against her to grab a handful of chips from the bag she held.

The warmth of him standing so close made her shiver.

"You can't be cold." His deep voice held a challenge.

"No." Far from it, but she'd never admit to what he did to her. What he'd always done. Clearing her throat, she managed to ask in a normal sounding voice, "What do you want on your sandwich? There's turkey, salami or ham."

"Salami and ham, please. I think there's sub rolls in there, too."

Monica looked at him. "So you want a sub?"

He grinned and grabbed another handful of chips. "Please. With lettuce, tomato and onion and Italian dressing. And provolone."

"Anything else?" Her voice dripped sarcasm.

He looked completely unrepentant. "That ought to do it, but if I think of something else, I'll let you know."

She pushed him out of her way and reached in the fridge to fetch the rolls and other ingredients needed. When she returned to the island counter, thankfully, Cash was gone.

He had moved into the living room, switching on the TV to the station that broadcast round-the-clock weather. "It's supposed to stay warm the next couple of days. Why don't we take the side-by-sides out to that waterfall near Munising?"

"Yeah!!!" Ethan cheered.

Owen grinned with a milk mustache.

"What if there are trees down along the route?" They could use the rugged trail opposite the driveway that ran north, the one they'd returned on yesterday.

Cash stretched out on the couch. "I'll take the chain saw with us. Worst case, we turn around and come back."

"Okay, sure, let's go," Monica agreed.

Anything was better than being cooped up on such a lovely day, and they needed a break from clearing the yard. And Monica needed a break from Cash. In the side-by-sides, they'd pretty much be apart for the rest of the afternoon.

Well, that didn't work out the way he'd planned. Cash stood next to the side-by-side, staring at another large tree that blocked their path to the waterfall. It was too large for the chain saw, which he'd wrapped in a heavy plastic bag and strapped into the back storage space.

So much for getting away from the cabin and Monica's feminine presence. She was a constant reminder of how nice it was having her around. Whether she made him a sandwich or shared coffee with him, she wrapped him in a sense of home that he liked far too much.

He rubbed his neck and then headed back to Monica and Owen. Bracing his arms against the roll bar of their utility vehicle, he explained the situation. "There's no getting through this way. We can take that smaller path we passed and see where it goes."

"I think we should head back. I'm cold and—" she gestured toward Owen "—I think he is, too."

"Got it." They'd hit several puddles on the way. Their jeans and shoes were all soaked, except for Monica's dry toes in her rubber boots. The warmth of midday was fleeting, as early evening crept upon them with a promise of a beautiful sunset.

"You lead." Monica nodded.

He grinned. "Always."

She grinned back.

Cash didn't know how he'd stay away from her when every inch of him wanted to hold her again. If he had those crayons handy, he'd cover a sheet of paper in softer colors ranging from blue to purplish pink. If only longing were as simple as the hues on a color chart.

For once, he drove slowly. He was in no hurry to return the cabin and face the temptation of holding Monica. The whole way back to the cabin, he inched along. Even through the mud puddles, he didn't floor it, but Ethan didn't seem to mind. He looked chilled, as well, and Cash was pretty sure neither boy would balk at the idea of a hot bath. Cash wouldn't either. His body ached from using the chain saw.

When they finally reached the cabin, the sun hung low in the sky. Parking the side-by-sides in the pole barn, they all moved a little slower than normal.

"I need a hot shower." Monica rubbed her bare arms.

None of them had bothered to put on the jackets they'd packed for the ride.

"Go ahead. I'll get the boys in the tub." Cash kicked off his wet tennis shoes at the back door, instructing his nephews to do the same.

Owen's teeth chattered.

"Come on, young'uns. Time to get clean and get warm." He looked at Monica. "We're going to drop these clothes in the washer, so if you don't mind…"

"Oh, sure thing." She dashed up the stairs.

He noticed that her socks were still white and dry. Why hadn't he thought to bring rain boots for the boys? "Okay, peel off everything and head for the bathroom," he told them.

Cash drew a bath, making sure the water wasn't too hot. He added some bubble bath and handed his nephews each a washcloth when they climbed in. "Scrub behind your ears."

He left the door open a crack and then went into his room and slipped into a different T-shirt and a pair of sweats. He'd shower after. Gathering up his dirty clothes along with the boys', he dumped the pile into the washer in the laundry room. Adding soap, he turned the knob for a heavy-duty wash and clicked start.

In the living room, he built a fire in the woodstove to chase away the chill. Late August nights grew nippy in the UP, announcing that fall was on their heels. Winter would soon follow and this part of the state saw its fair share of snow.

Part of him missed Michigan, with its distinct seasons. Growing up in the northwest "Tip of the Mitt", he'd looked forward to snow. He liked to ski, loved to snowmobile and as he recalled, he'd enjoyed quite a few snowball fights in his day. He'd even thrown his share of packed white stuff at Monica. She'd retaliate with a thrown snowball or punch to his arm. He remembered that she had a pretty good right hook, too.

Hearing footsteps, he looked up to see Monica descending the loft stairs. Her long blond hair was wet, her face scrubbed clean, and she wore a white, long-sleeved T-shirt over soft gray sweats that made her legs look a mile long. He sucked in a breath of air as if a fist had punched his midsection.

She made straight for the woodstove and held out her hands to it. "The fire feels nice, thanks. Are the boys still in the tub?"

Cash chuckled at the sound of splashing coming from the bathroom. "Ah, yeah. I better check on them."

"I'll get dinner started if you want to shower upstairs."

He cocked his head. "I can skip it and help with dinner."

She made a face and fanned her nose. "You should rethink that."

"That bad?" He was used to going without a shower for days while deployed or in training exercises. Not a big deal.

"Well." Monica scrunched her nose. "Uh, yeah."

He laughed and walked toward the bathroom, grabbed

a towel and snapped it in the air. "Okay, boys, outta that tub and into warm pajamas. My turn to shower."

He helped them dry off, but then his nephews squealed and ran bare-bottomed into their room, laughing the whole way.

Cash couldn't believe the tub water was so dirty that, once drained, it left behind a filthy ring. He'd have to clean this place pretty good before his mom and sister-in-law arrived.

By the time he jumped out of the shower, the smell of something really good reached his nostrils, causing his stomach to rumble. He changed quickly and met Monica near the stove.

Peeking over her shoulder, he breathed in sautéed chicken with peppers and onions. "Smells amazing."

"It's going to be fajitas." She elbowed him out of the way and fetched a can of refried beans from the pantry.

"When did you learn to cook?"

She gave him a look as if he'd asked the silliest question on Earth. "I've always cooked. All of us kids learned how."

"What can I do?"

She shook her head. "Stay out of my way."

"Yes, ma'am." He saluted, went to the fridge and grabbed a beverage. Snapping open the tab, he checked on his nephews, who were now sprawled on the couch watching TV.

A soft rosy glow from the low sun tinged the treetops outside. The sun set earlier now with the close of summer. The small logs had caught fire in the woodstove, giving off the warm glow of hearth and home. No lights were on inside, other than the one over the stove.

He slipped onto a stool at the island counter and

watched Monica as she mixed a can of creamed corn into a bowl of corn muffin mix. This felt like home. She had always been part of home for him.

"Cornbread too, huh?" He took another pull from the can.

"Why not?"

"Right, why not?" Just then his cell phone rang and vibrated in his pocket. "Hello?"

"Cash? I'm still working on getting a team over there but it all depends on how Monday goes."

"I understand. Want to talk to the boys?"

"Please." His sister-in-law sounded like she missed them. Of course she would.

Cash handed over the phone to Ethan, who'd jumped up and now stood next to him. "Talk to your mom."

"Hi, Mom. Yep, that lady is still here." Ethan glanced at Monica and then moved over to the couch. "Yeah, we're being good…"

Cash turned to Monica. How many days would they be stuck here? "She's working on getting a team here as soon as possible."

Monica briefly closed her eyes. "Good. That's good."

"Yeah." It couldn't be soon enough, and yet in a way he didn't care when they came, because he actually enjoyed this. Spending this much time with Monica, he knew he'd miss her once she left.

He'd miss her real bad. And that wasn't good.

Chapter Nine

After dinner, Monica wiped off the table. "Do you guys want to go outside for a campfire?"

The boys lounged on the couch watching TV, and Cash was looking at his phone. No one responded.

"Campfire?" she repeated.

Cash looked up. "We gathered enough wood this morning and we'll be doing more tomorrow, so I think we're over it for now."

She couldn't believe three males preferred to remain indoors on a glorious, albeit chilly, evening. Who knew how long they'd be stuck here, and the TV would always be an option. Hunting in the same closet where she'd found the crayons, Monica pulled out some games. "What about checkers, chess or cards? Oh, and we also have The Game of Life."

Ethan took one look at the colorful box of the board game and pointed. "That one."

Monica glanced at Cash. "Owen might have a hard time with it, but we can help him out."

"Sure." He shrugged and yawned. "For a while, anyway."

"Everything okay?" She nodded toward his phone.

"Yeah, just checking in with my superiors."

Monica chewed her bottom lip. His leave would be up soon and he looked as if he couldn't wait to return. She could see it in his eyes. Cash loved being a marine and that wasn't ever going to change.

She opened the box and laid the board out on the table. Then she organized the various cards, little cars, people pegs and money. "Choose your colors."

Owen grabbed a blue car.

"I wanted that one." Ethan reached for it.

Owen swept his arm away from his brother.

Cash stalled an argument waiting to happen with a firm voice. "Choose another one."

Ethan glared at his little brother and took the green car.

Owen stuck out his tongue.

Cash looked at Monica as if he was tired of the boys' bickering. "What color do you want?"

She smiled sweetly. "I'll take yellow."

He chose the red car and handed her a pink peg. He and the boys each took a blue peg. "Monica, why don't you start us off?"

She spun the wheel and moved her car along the spaces heading to college, borrowing money from the bank to pay for tuition.

Cash raised an eyebrow. "You've already gone that route. Why not try a different path and start off your career?"

"I liked college. Are you going to go my way and try a different path?"

He headed toward starting a career. "Nope, might as well play it the same way I have in real life."

Monica spread the career cards out in front of Cash. He picked an athlete with a large salary. "Sixty thousand? Seriously?"

He grinned. "And you're already in debt."

The start of this game actually mirrored their own lives. Cash had gone straight to the marines, earning a wage right off the bat, while Monica had graduated from college with a hefty student loan even though her parents had helped out with her tuition. She'd paid off that student loan when she refinanced the small home she'd bought a few years ago to make over her single-car garage into an office.

Ethan took his turn, choosing to follow his uncle to a career. His first career card required a college degree, so he had to choose again. He drew a salesman card and received his cash salary. "What does a salesman do?"

"He sells stuff, like cars or houses," Cash explained.

"I wanna sell cars." Ethan said, and spun the wheel and landed on a bill to pay. "No fair!"

"That's life." Monica and Cash said it in unison, and then they both laughed.

Ethan frowned, not getting the joke.

Owen finally took his turn, and it was no surprise that he followed her to college and into debt.

They played for half an hour or so, laughing and teasing when each of them had to stop and get married. Monica was the first to land on a baby space. She knew this was only a game, but the reminder that in real life she might never have the chance to experience having a child cut deep.

Her fingers remained on her car and she scrunched her nose, trying to shake off those gloomy thoughts. "Dare I look? Is it a pink or blue peg?"

Cash narrowed his gaze. "Which would you prefer?"

Monica wouldn't care if she had a boy or girl, as long as the baby was healthy. As long as she had that possibility.

She locked onto his dark gray eyes and held out her hand. "Give me a baby girl."

His face paled.

Monica had only been playing along and yet her stomach tipped and rolled at the look of sheer panic on his face. As if she'd asked him to have a child with her for real.

"It's just a game." She gave a shaky laugh, but the idea had already been planted and was taking root as what she wanted.

No. No way.

Marriage to Cash meant standing by helpless when he left for deployments. A marine in a Special Operations Command company had assignments that came quickly and often. Cash would be off to who knew where half the time. She couldn't handle that. Even if her future was stable, she didn't want the kind of uncertainty that came with a military life.

Cash finally looked away and stood. "It's a dumb game and I'm done with it."

"Aw, come on, Uncle Cash." Ethan slumped.

Owen had already sneaked away to the couch and turned on the TV with a click of the remote.

"You two keep playing. I'm going to get some air. Kind of stuffy in here."

Monica traded a glance with Ethan.

The eight-year-old shrugged, looking glum. "Game over."

"Checkers?" she offered.

"Nah. I'll watch TV with Owen." He stood, too, then thought better of leaving the table. "Want help putting it away?"

Monica smiled at him, her heart full. He'd become a helper this weekend. "No, that's okay, but thank you for offering."

He gave her a nod.

It was the sort of gesture Cash might have given and it made her ache. There was no escaping the way that man made her feel this weekend.

In the midst of gathering up the cars and pulling out each peg, Monica glanced out the slider door. She spotted Cash standing on the deck looking up at the dark sky. He was so good at hiding his feelings, but that look of panic had been pretty clear. He did not want a wife or a family of his own.

She had no idea how he really felt about her. He cared, sure. He might even be attracted to her. Sometimes, she'd catch a look of longing in his eyes only to see it shuttered up quickly, leaving Monica to wonder if she'd imagined seeing it.

"Monica, get out here with the boys." Cash stuck his head back in the door and switched off the kitchen light. "Come quick."

Monica looked at the boys and they looked at her. Then they all jumped up and ran for the deck. Monica grabbed a couple throw blankets from off the couch before stepping outside.

"What is it?" she whispered when she was on the deck, in case there was an animal Cash didn't want spooked. The thought that a black bear might be roaming around sent a chill through her. Would he really bring the boys outside to see it?

Cash pointed toward the north. "There, along the horizon. See the colors? It's the northern lights."

The boys both stood still as stones, completely transfixed at the magnificent sight.

Monica's mouth dropped open as she stared. Shimmers of neon green and purple danced in the sky, making waves of translucent color. "Wow."

Cash pulled her by the hand, leading her down the steps. "How many blankets do you have there?"

"Two. But they aren't full-size."

"I'll grab a couple more and douse the rest of the inside lights." He was gone before she could refuse.

Of course they couldn't let this opportunity pass by, even if it meant spreading blankets on the cold, damp grass away from the house in order to get a good view of the northern sky. She'd make sure the boys were between them, because huddling under a blanket next to Cash Miller seemed like a bad idea.

Cash made his way in the darkness. He'd turned off every light in the cabin save for a night-light in the bathroom that stayed on for the boys. Hoisting an old quilt and a woolen blanket he'd found in the linen closet, he followed the sound of giggles.

The boys each had one of the small blankets wrapped around them, and Monica stood close to them. She rested a hand on each of their shoulders as if protecting them from whatever might come out of the woods beyond the high grass.

Monica.

Even though it was only a board game they'd been playing, the idea of giving Monica a baby girl had hit him hard. She got to him. She'd always gotten to him, sneaking her way down deep into his heart and making him want things he'd be better off without. Having a family of his own meant going into each mission with a desire to save his own skin. That was deadly thinking. His job was worrying about his men making it in and out alive.

"Here." He awkwardly draped the woolen blanket around her, careful not to touch her.

She held on to the edges and watched while he spread the huge quilt on the ground.

He lay on top of the quilt and opened his arms. "Somebody cover me up."

The boys each launched themselves onto him. Owen settled into his left armpit and Ethan wiggled into the crook of his right arm.

Cash looked up at Monica. "Are you going to lie down so we can watch the sky?"

She gave him a goofy-looking half smile and knelt down, covering all of them with the woolen blanket before lying back. "Wow, look at those colors."

They all gazed upward. The sky seemed to brighten with a wash of new greens and purples and even some blue. The lights moved like waves over the dark sky, dipping and rolling up from behind the tops of the trees.

"Why does it do that?" Ethan asked.

"Geomagnetic storms on the sun." Cash folded his right arm behind his head.

"I like to think that God is showing us that He's real. That He's with us." Monica shifted lower so the blanket reached her neck.

"Cold?" Cash asked.

"I'm good."

He could just barely see her breath. "Get closer. Roll back into me, Owen."

The little guy snuggled as directed.

Monica inched closer and buried her bare feet under the leg of Cash's sweats.

He yelped and sucked in his breath. Her icy toes shot a shiver through him. "Where's your shoes?"

"I had flip-flops on."

Owen giggled and shifted closer to Monica.

She wrapped her arm around the tyke, which put her elbow against the side of Cash's waist. The warmth of that small connection seared through his shirt, setting his skin on fire.

"Do you think my dad can see these?" Ethan stared straight up at the sky.

Cash was trying to get beyond the sensation of Monica's feet against his calves and elbow in his side. Without thinking, he responded honestly. "I don't know, Ethan. Maybe."

The boy wasn't bothered by that answer. "I hope so, because it's really cool."

"It is." Cash turned his head and slammed into Monica's gaze.

He didn't look away and neither did she. She might as well be a truck winch, pulling him in. He reached out and gathered up a handful of her long hair, feeling the silky strength of it. He brought the strands to his face and inhaled the scent of her.

Her eyes watched him, then suddenly clouded over with sadness. She turned her head away, blocking his view of whatever she might be thinking.

What was going on with her? Maybe that guy meant more to her than she'd let on. Cash let go of her hair and slipped his hand under her neck to give her what he hoped was an encouraging squeeze.

She brought her other hand up to meet his and held on.

He shifted closer in order to thread his fingers through hers. Whatever it was, he wanted her to know that he cared. Maybe too much, considering that he couldn't quite erase the idea of Monica with a baby girl from his mind.

The four of them lay there watching the northern lights until nature's show finally dimmed into nothing.

"That was so cool," Ethan whispered.

"I know." Cash glanced at Owen. The kid's eyes were closed.

"Uncle Cash?"

"Yeah?"

"Why'd my dad die?"

Cash had asked that same question a hundred times. He could give the pat answer that sometimes bad things happened to good people, but he didn't want Ethan to ever fear death. It was bad for the rest of them, but death wasn't bad for Cole. His brother was in a better place. "I don't know, Ethan. I do know he's with God and happy."

"It's not fair." His voice sounded thin and watery.

"It's not for us, because we're left behind to miss him. I know." He felt Monica squeeze his fingers. "But God's with us, too. Monica's right. The Lord showed us those lights tonight because He understands exactly how we feel."

Ethan didn't respond.

Cash knew the kid was thinking. Thinking hard.

"When will it feel better?"

Like a punch to the gut, Cash didn't want to lie about that one, either. It had been nearly twenty years since his own father had died and it still hurt at times. Times like these.

"You'll always miss your dad, Ethan. And I'll always miss my brother, but with time the hurt won't be so sharp."

"Oh."

Just then a shooting star whizzed across the sky.

"Did you see that?" Ethan pointed.

"I sure did." Cash had the odd sense that he'd been given a sign somehow. That shooting star reminded him that God was indeed trustworthy, even when things seemed so unfair.

Owen sat up, looking lost and sleepy.

Monica sat up, too. "It's getting late. I think I'm going to call it a night."

"Good idea. Let's go, guys. Bathroom then bed." Cash stood, and he and Monica gathered up the blankets.

"I'll take care of these while you get the boys tucked in." She took the blankets from him after they stepped inside the cabin.

The heat of indoors surrounded him like a warm hug. As he watched Monica fold the blankets, it hit him that being here together felt disturbingly right. Worse, he didn't really care when the logging team came to clear the driveway.

She shook out the quilt and headed for the laundry room. "I'll just throw this in the dryer for a few minutes to get the damp out."

"Yeah." He remained rooted in place while the boys ducked into the bathroom.

With a sinking feeling, he realized he didn't want to

admit the obvious. Monica had always been the woman for him. He'd known it for years and yet couldn't pull that trigger. He'd never even tried, except for the night he'd kissed her all those years ago. That one kiss had shaken him to the core and he'd kept his distance from her ever since.

Had he missed the mark by remaining alone all these years without once trying to pursue her? If so, what should he do about it now? Even if he did do something about it, how could he effectively remain a soldier?

Monica threw a dryer sheet in with the quilt, set the timer for twenty minutes and hit Start. That should freshen it up while it dried. When she came out of the laundry room, Cash was still standing in the same place and he looked confused.

"You okay?" His conversation with Ethan about Cole's death had torn her heart in two.

"Yeah, why?" He didn't look fine. He looked troubled, worried, and some of that panic from earlier still lingered in his eyes.

"You're just standing there."

He ran his hand through his hair. "Just waiting on the boys. Want to help me tuck them in?"

"Sure. Let me know when they're in their pj's and I'll be in." Monica stashed the woolen blanket in the linen closet and tossed the throws on the back of the couch.

Glancing at the woodstove, she rubbed her arms. The fire had burned down to nothing. No use starting a new one, as she'd probably fall asleep on the couch if she had to wait up for the flames to die down before going to bed.

She looked at the clock in the kitchen. It was only ten, so surely Cash would stay up for a little while yet.

She heard giggles and the snap of a towel from the boys' room, along with Cash's voice teasing them.

Maybe just a small fire.

Opening the woodstove door, she stuffed the thinnest kindling inside until it caught from the meager coals inside. Once the flames flared to life, she threw in the smallest logs from the wood box and stared as the flames shimmied and grew brighter.

"We're ready," Cash called out.

"Be right there." She closed and locked the woodstove door, reveling in the heat for a moment.

Entering the boys' room, she smiled. Ethan was curled up on the top bunk. Owen had the bottom. "You guys look pretty snug."

"Snug as two bugs." Ethan grinned.

"Let's pray and then lights out." Cash took Ethan's hand and offered her his other one.

Monica gladly took it, enjoying the feel of tough calluses on his palm. Cash had strong hands. He was a strong man. He didn't shy away from his nephews' grief or trying to help them through it. She reached for Owen's hand, bowed her head and waited for Cash to pray.

His words were simple, requesting a good night's sleep for all of them and peace in the coming days.

Peace.

Monica could use a whole lot of that. She wasn't at peace with her diagnosis, her treatment options or her deepening feelings for Cash. Everything seemed jumbled together and she couldn't see how any of it would turn out good.

"Amen," Cash whispered.

"Amen," Ethan said.

Owen merely nodded.

"Good night." Monica gave each boy a soft tap to the nose. "See you in the morning."

Cash followed her, leaving the door open only a crack. "Thanks."

"For what?"

"For being you." He passed her and headed for the living room. "You made up a fire. Nice."

It was blazing now, bringing a cheery glow to the dark room. The only other light shone from over the stove in the kitchen, where she'd clicked it on after they'd come in.

She followed him even though she should say goodnight and head for the loft.

He opened the woodstove door and threw in another log, a bigger one. One that would take a while to burn down. "You know, that day I took the boys out for ice cream, I prayed for help. I needed it."

Monica slipped onto the couch, tucking her still-cold-and-bare feet underneath her. "This is a good thing you're doing, bringing the boys here, talking to them honestly about their dad."

Cash closed the woodstove and sat down next to her. "It wasn't but a few minutes after that prayer that I saw your car parked in the driveway. God answered me with you."

Her stomach flipped, but she kept her voice even, hoping Cash didn't see what this was doing to her. Falling for those boys. Falling for him. "Glad I could help. They're sweet."

"What if there's more to it than that, more than just

them? What if that downed tree was a way to keep you here?"

Monica laughed. "Are you saying that I wasn't supposed to leave?"

"Maybe not yet. What's going on with you, Monica? Maybe I can help you like you've helped me."

She stared into his earnest gray eyes, wishing he could help her, but there was nothing Cash could do. She cupped his cheek. "Thanks, but some things a person has to work through on their own."

He leaned into her palm and turned to place a brief kiss on the inside of her wrist. "What kinds of things?"

Monica should pull her hand back, but Cash was making her head spin.

He curled his other arm around her waist and drew her even closer.

"Cash, we're not kids anymore." She braced her free hand against his chest, ready to push him back, but feeling the strong beats of his heart, she stalled.

Would kissing him again after all these years be different or the same? It might be like coming home after a long absence, and that's what worried her. Cash felt a whole lot like her *one and only,* but falling in love wouldn't do either of them any good.

"So?" His voice was dangerously low and sweet.

"So?" She glared at him. Nothing had changed for them and yet everything had changed. "So, you don't want any distractions."

"Maybe I'm rethinking that."

Monica's heart skipped with hope.

She shouldn't get her hopes up, but she could barely breathe, let alone respond as she watched his dear face move closer.

She closed her eyes even though she knew better. She didn't stop him from settling his lips on hers even though she knew she should. Even though there could be no happy ending for them, she wanted this. What harm could there be in having just one more kiss to treasure, one more to savor?

He kissed her softly, tentatively at first, holding back as if wrestling with his doubts.

Monica wrestled with hers, too. She wanted this moment too much to let doubt steal a special memory from her. Throwing caution to the wind, she deepened the kiss.

Cash tightened his hold and responded with an intensity that sent her heart racing. One kiss blurred into another and another. Each one better than the one before.

And then suddenly, he pulled back.

"Cash?" she whispered.

He sat back and ran his hand through his hair. "Look, I'm sorry. I shouldn't have done that."

"Why—" Her voice, a mere whisper, broke. The rest of her words were stuck in her throat.

He stood, looking tense and full of regret. "Good night, Monica."

She nodded. There was really nothing more to say.

They had teetered close to a place that could ruin a good friendship and he'd pulled them back to safety.

Only she didn't feel so safe with her heart exposed. Sadness threatened to crush her because she wanted a life with Cash.

But a life spent with Cash would be far from safe with him going into harm's way. It was beyond unfair to saddle him with her health situation after he'd just lost his brother. She couldn't send him back to his company worried about her, so she vowed not to tell him about the cancer.

Not now.

Maybe not ever.

Chapter Ten

The next morning, Cash lay in bed staring at the ceiling. The relationship between him and Monica might as well have been a hurricane that blew in from the Atlantic, destroying everything in its path. She'd cut a swath of longing to make a real home and family with her that would be hard to shake, even after he left.

He'd been curious to see if a simple kiss would have the same impact as it did all those years ago. Not only had it been a bad move on his part, but he'd messed up big time by apologizing. One thing had remained the same—there was nothing simple about his feelings for her.

Kissing Monica once might not have been wise, but kissing her again and again had been stupid. He'd never forget the look on her face after he'd abruptly pulled away from her. She'd appeared hurt and disappointed, and so tempting that he'd had to bolt fast. Saying he was sorry had only made matters worse.

It had been a big fat crock, too. He wasn't sorry for kissing her. He was sorry for not being the kind of man she deserved. The kind who'd always be around.

He got up, hit the head and then made his bed in usual tight marine style. Padding out of his room, he froze when he saw Monica in the kitchen quietly making coffee. Her hair hung long and loose, and his fingers twitched to dive in and grab handfuls of the silky strands. She wore an oversize sweater that he guessed she'd pulled out of one of the closets. It was way too big to be hers.

He finally made his presence known. "You're up early."

She turned, startled. Her face flushed a pretty pink and then she quickly looked away, scooping ground coffee into a filter. "Morning."

Great. Just great. Things were awkward between them now. What else did he expect? He walked to the sliding glass door and looked out. The sun hadn't yet risen, but the eastern sky was brightening and the ground showed patches of light frost. "It got cold overnight."

"Yes, it did." Her voice sounded too soft.

Cash closed his eyes and mentally kicked himself a hundred times over. He hoped the cold overnight temps didn't slow down the tree service guys. "I'll get a fire going."

"Would you like breakfast?"

He headed for the woodstove without looking at her. "Not yet."

The coffee maker gurgled and hissed.

He could smell the luscious brew and even that didn't help dispel his regret. He knew better than to tell a woman he was sorry for kissing her. Especially this woman. He knew Monica well enough to understand she'd taken his act of self-restraint as something wrong with her.

There was nothing wrong with her. She was perfect.

He, on the other hand, had baggage that should stay packed. "Monica, about last night…"

"Don't." She held up her hand as she slipped into a chair near the woodstove. "It's okay. I get it."

Did she? "What do you get?"

She glared at him. "You want me to spell it out?"

"Yeah. I do."

She cocked a perfectly shaped eyebrow. "You don't want an emotional encumbrance and I don't want to be… I don't want a military life."

She didn't want to be the wife of a *Raider*. He couldn't say that he blamed her. She grew up with a father who had retired from a lifelong career in the army and her oldest brother had been an army captain before he'd gotten out. She knew what to expect and what he'd expect of her—to buck up and take it when he left.

He gave her a crooked grin and tried to lighten the moment. "So, you don't want me."

Her eyes grew wide and then she laughed. "That's right, Cash. I don't want you."

He loved her laugh, even though her eyes told him the exact opposite. He'd be better off not looking into those brilliant blues of hers, so he focused on building a fire.

When he finally heard the last hiss announcing that coffee was ready, he still didn't stop snapping kindling even as Monica passed by him.

He clenched his jaw as the scent of her swirled around him like one of those smoke fingers from a cartoon enticing him to move closer, only to get burned.

Stuffing a couple small logs on top of the twigs, he struck a long match and lit the wood, waiting for it to catch. It wasn't a long wait. The snap and crackle and smell of burning wood soothed, somewhat.

"Here." Monica handed him a mug of black coffee, then took a seat near the woodstove. This morning she wore socks. Slouchy looking things that pooled around her slender ankles.

"Thanks." He shut the woodstove door and stood, sipping his coffee. "It's good."

"Thanks."

He sat on the couch and took another sip. He'd miss this. He'd miss her. More than he'd ever thought possible.

They didn't say anything more as they drank their coffee and stared at the flames through the thick glass door of the woodstove. Cash hoped the boys would soon get up, so they'd have some kind of buffer that might return them to normal.

After last night, he wasn't sure they'd ever return to normal. They'd crossed into perilous territory and there might be no going back.

Monica finished her coffee and looked up as a yawning Owen entered the family room. Ethan wasn't far behind. "Morning, fellas."

"Morning." Ethan threw himself on the couch.

She grinned at them both, glad they were up. "I don't know about you guys, but I'm hungry for breakfast."

"Me, too!" Ethan fist pumped the air.

Owen reached for her as she headed for the kitchen. Monica bent down and hugged him. When she straightened, her gaze slammed into Cash, who was watching her.

He gave her a nod and quickly looked away. Grabbing the poker, he made like he was busy stoking the fire.

Why did she keep doing that? Looking for him and at him as if she couldn't get enough of him? She couldn't help that she'd fallen in love with Cash Miller over this weekend. She'd known him a long time, knew he was a man of integrity and strong faith. What she hadn't known was how wonderful he was with his nephews and that she could trust him. Really trust him. He was a man she could lean on, that's for sure.

Could she trust him with her cancer news? She knew she could, but didn't know if she should. It was beyond tempting to unload her fears, but she didn't want to send him off with worries that might get in the way of his safe return back home. She gripped the side of the sink at the very idea of Cash getting hurt because of her.

It was better to leave it alone. And leave the idea of them as a couple alone, too. It'd be too hard to make it work when they both faced uncertainty. Last night might have been amazing, but it was terrifying at the same time. She'd never experienced with anyone else what she'd felt with Cash.

"What are you going to make?" Ethan slipped onto the stool on the other side of the island.

Monica turned and smiled. "How about eggs and bacon and potatoes."

Ethan looked skeptical. "Potatoes?"

Monica laughed. The boy was obviously thinking the mashed variety. "Fried, you know, like hash browns."

"Oh."

Potatoes were her go-to comfort food and Monica needed all the comfort she could get, especially when she didn't know how long she'd be stuck here. If she could, she'd snag a side-by-side and drive it all the way home.

After breakfast, of course.

"Want some help?" Cash moved in.

The kitchen was open concept, but the lane between the appliances and the island was tight. He'd get in her way. They might even bump into each other— "Sure."

Monica reached into the bottom crisper of the fridge and pulled out a small of bag of potatoes she'd brought. She plopped it in front of Cash. "Peel these."

He looked at her.

"Please." She smiled, not realizing how sharp she'd sounded.

It wasn't his fault she loved him. Okay, maybe it was, especially after last night. Monica would never forget the feel of his lips on hers—testing and tasting. Then there was the reverent way he'd threaded his fingers through her hair, grabbing hold of it as if trying its strength, only to then kiss the strands as if they were spun gold.

Her stomach twisted. She'd lose her hair. She might lose even more. How would Cash take all that? Would he look at her the same way? Or would it be different? What if he was repulsed by her scarred body?

What if she was?

Tears burned at the corners of her eyes.

She reached into the fridge again, grappling with her emotions, glad that Ethan and Owen were helping Cash. He'd found two peelers for them while he used a paring knife. The chore was perfect for keeping all three males busy, especially one male. She didn't want Cash noticing her heightened sense of sorrow.

She grabbed the eggs and a bowl and cracked them hard.

Please, Lord...

She didn't know what to pray anymore. She just

wanted to go home, meet with the doctors and get it all over and done with.

She felt a hand cup her elbow and looked up.

Cash.

He gave her a long, searching look.

She wanted to look away but couldn't. She'd miss his face, even whiskered. Maybe especially with the scraggly beard that made him look even more rugged. Holding her breath, she simply stared.

"Bacon?"

She furrowed her brow and breathed in. "Huh?"

"Don't you think we should get going on the bacon?"

"Oh. Yeah." Monica reached in the lower cupboard for a large frying pan.

Cash handed her the package of bacon with a teasing gleam in his eyes. "Maybe I should take over."

Monica elbowed him aside. "Not a chance. Now get out of my way."

"Come on, boys, let's watch the morning weather and plan our day."

Monica didn't know how he did it, but he'd put her in a box and shelved her. Shelved *them* as in not now and maybe not ever. Smart guy. There was a good reason he'd remained single all this time. He could shut off his feelings like he turned off a light.

She knew he cared about her and it was more than mere friendship. His agitated apology for kissing her hinted that maybe those feelings ran deep. She might be an idiot, but she wasn't stupid. She just wished she had some of his skill in compartmentalizing everything and everyone.

She peeked at him again, and he caught her.

She quickly looked away and focused on laying strips

of bacon in the hot pan. Hearing the sizzle and pop, she was only too happy to prepare a hearty breakfast. It might keep her mind occupied. After that, she had to check in with her assistant and let her know what was going on, and then there were more branches and limbs to clean up.

All busy work that wouldn't erase the fact that her heart was silently breaking.

After dinner, Cash considered the long stretch of another cool night ahead and cringed. What on earth were they going to do to pass the evening?

The day had been fine as he and Monica had gone their separate ways. After the morning dishes were done, he took the boys for a walk in the woods to see more downed trees and storm damage. He wanted to give Monica a quiet space to get some work done. She'd said she needed to check in with clients.

After a light lunch, they'd all pitched in to clear the rest of the branches in the yard and driveway. He'd used the chain saw on another small tree and stacked the wood. Finishing that, they came inside for an early dinner of plain hot dogs for the boys, while he and Monica had made elaborate chili dogs with fajita leftovers from the previous night. It was only five o'clock and they were done eating, with nothing but time and a long stretch of night ahead.

He came out from cleaning the mess of a downstairs bathroom and caught Monica wiping down the kitchen table. Tomorrow loomed wide open, as well. How long were they going to be stuck here? He needed to leave no later than Saturday morning to drive back to base in order to report for duty on Monday. He had a twenty-two hour drive to reach Camp Lejeune in southern North Carolina.

Monica looked at him and laughed.

"What?"

"Afraid you'll get your hands dirty?"

"So I wear rubber gloves when I clean a bathroom. Those cleaners are harsh." He'd picked up the habit of wearing them when he'd been in boot camp and assigned to clean the latrine. He'd been *asked* to repeat that duty on a couple occasions for disciplinary reasons.

She held up her hand. "Don't put those back under the kitchen sink. They belong to the bathroom now."

He stripped them off and stashed the gloves in the cabinet under the bathroom sink. Walking toward Monica, he spread his hands wide, "What now?"

She glanced at the boys on the couch watching TV, before looking at him. Her eyes seemed to glow. "Campfire?"

He shook his head. "Too early."

"We can burn the tops of those trees you cut up. That's better done in daylight."

"What's with you and fire?"

Her cheeks flushed again. "Best part of yard cleanup."

She'd become a living wildfire to him, scorching his memory. The taste of her was forever burned into him and this time he didn't think he could shake it.

He turned to the boys. "You guys want to burn some wood?"

Ethan jumped up. "Yeah!"

Owen looked reluctant. Cash couldn't blame the kid

for wanting to stay indoors rather than work. They'd already put in a lot of cleanup hours.

Cash finger-combed his whiskered chin. "I bet there's more caterpillars for you to find outside."

Owen perked up.

"You don't have help with the wood if you don't want to."

The little guy nodded and got off the couch.

"Shoes and a jacket," Cash said.

Owen marched into his room along with Ethan.

"Thank you." Monica perched on the lower steps of the loft.

It hit him that he'd do just about anything for her. "You're welcome."

"I'll grab a sweatshirt and meet you outside."

Cash nodded, and hearing Ethan's raised voice, headed for the boys' room. "Come on, guys, what's wrong now?"

"He won't give me my jacket." Ethan pointed at Owen.

Cash looked at Owen, the little instigator. "Hand it over."

Owen gave his brother the jacket. The gleam of mischief in his eyes warned Cash that whatever was going on between the two wasn't over.

"Now your shoes."

His sister-in-law had had the foresight to send work boots with her boys. Since their tennis shoes were still wet from riding the side-by-sides, the boys had worn their work boots on this morning's walk. Cash grabbed one of Owen's boots and helped the boy into it, then the other, lacing them up.

He glanced at Ethan, who'd managed to get his on

just fine but needed help tying them. "Now jackets and let's go."

Cash grabbed a long-sleeved pullover that he slipped on over his T-shirt on the way out. The early evening had turned rather chilly with a bank of cloud cover that had moved in, but it wasn't as cold as the night before. They might be in for more rain.

Monica joined them. She wore her rubber boots and grabbed work gloves from the pole barn.

He couldn't help but watch her fluid movements as she walked toward him.

"Gloves? I know how you worry about getting your hands dirty." Monica gave him a teasing smile.

He took the pair she offered and pulled on her ponytail when she turned to help Ethan into a set.

"Ow." She swung around and cocked her fist, ready to give him a punch to the arm.

He ducked away.

She came after him, so he ran. It felt good to fall back into their old antics. It felt normal.

Ethan cheered and Cash could hear Owen's giggle as Monica chased him around the backyard. They played their own private game of tag. He'd stop, only to dart away again, but she caught up to him. Monica grabbed his shirt, he spun too fast and she slipped. They both fell, but Cash twisted so he brought Monica down to land on top of him when they hit the ground. The soft grassy earth wouldn't have hurt her, though.

He looked up into her startled face and grinned. "Cozy."

She squirmed and pushed against his chest. "Let me up."

He heard the breathlessness in her voice and that com-

fortable teasing they'd just reclaimed went up in flames.
She was on fire again, burning him, too, as he tightened
his hold on her. He studied her mouth. Could he get away
with a brief—?

"Don't you dare," she hissed.

He smirked. "I'm always up for a dare."

Too late. He heard peals of laughter as both boys
joined the pile by launching onto them.

Monica slid from his grasp as he loosened his hold
to roll and tickle Owen.

The boy squealed and laughed some more.

Ethan jumped on his back.

Cash got up with Ethan clinging to his shoulders and
Owen wrapped around his leg. He walked like Frankenstein toward Monica, who was pulling grass from her
hair. "Er-r-r…"

She looked at him and laughed. "Nice. Come on, we
have tree tops to burn."

"Fire bad." He continued with the Frankenstein voice,
but there was truth in what he said. He didn't want this
fire between him and Monica. It made it that much
harder to stay away from her. It would make saying
goodbye even worse.

The boys laughed. Owen rode his foot and Ethan
wrapped his legs around Cash's waist to stay on.

Just then his cell phone buzzed from within the mid-
thigh side pocket of his cargo pants. He gently flipped
Ethan over and onto the ground, and grabbed his phone.
"Yeah?"

"Cash, good news. A team will be there at first light
to get the driveway cleared. Your mom and I will be
there by lunchtime."

His heart sank as he glanced at Monica.

She tipped her head, looking concerned.

"Um, yeah, that's good. Monica will be glad. Hey, I have two monkeys climbing on me who want to talk to you."

"Is Owen—"

He cut her off. "No. Not yet."

He heard his sister-in-law sigh. "Okay, put them on."

He handed the phone to Ethan.

"Hi, Mom…"

Cash stepped toward Monica. "They're coming to clear that tree first thing in the morning."

Was it his imagination or did her eyes grow dim?

"Oh, okay. Good." She gave him a wan smile.

This was it. Tomorrow they'd say their goodbyes and go their own ways. It was what they wanted, wasn't it? Not really, not for him. He didn't want that at all, but it's what had to be.

He stepped closer. "Last night together. What do you want to do?"

She didn't look away from him. "Burn these, then maybe some sparklers. They're in the cabin somewhere. The boys might have fun with those."

He slapped his forehead. "I have more."

"More sparklers?"

"No. Fireworks," he whispered. "I brought them to set off on the last night with the boys, but I think tonight would be better."

With her.

This was their last night together and he wanted to make it memorable, but he didn't want to do anything that might jeopardize the solid friendship they already had.

"I don't know, Cash. Will it be safe?"

He laughed. "I've blown up a lot of stuff, so I can handle a few fireworks."

More truth, but could he handle the fireworks simmering between him and Monica?

Chapter Eleven

Monica watched the limb pile burn from a respectable distance, but she could still feel the heat. "Don't get too close. Owen, here, come by me."

Owen backed up and stood next to her.

It hadn't taken long for the leafy section of the pile to catch fire. The boys had cheered at the height of the flames shooting up into the sky. It was way higher than their little bonfire the other night. She didn't want either of them to trip or fall anywhere near the blaze.

Ethan was sticking pretty close to Cash.

She'd heard the eight-year-old utter "this is so cool" at least a handful of times.

They'd built the huge pile well away from the cabin, in a wide patch of tall grass before the woods started. Cash had doused the still-green treetops with a little gas before throwing a match to get it started. He'd reminded her of a mad scientist circling the pile and drizzling it with gas from a little tin can. Now, they simply viewed the huge inferno from far enough away, in awe.

She glanced at Cash, who was staring into the flames

with a crooked grin on his face. He loved it, too. Just like the boys. He looked up, caught her gaze and held it.

This was her last night at the cabin with Cash and his nephews. Bittersweet on so many levels, but the biggest takeaway was that Monica wanted a family of her own more than she ever had before. Maybe because of the risks that came with chemotherapy and the possibility of coming out on the other side with fertility issues. All that seemed amplified and way more real after this weekend. She truly ached for what she might not have.

It would also be the last time she'd see Cash Miller for a long, long while, and that hurt more than she'd thought possible.

He gave her a slight smile as if he could read her thoughts, and his expression turned somber.

"Can we roast marshmallows?" Ethan asked.

Monica laughed at the idea of trying to toast a puny marshmallow next to this inferno. "Maybe later."

"After it burns down, we'll rake the coals into a smaller pile. It'll be perfect then." Cash had the better answer.

How long would that be? They'd been outside for at least an hour or so finishing up the limb pile. The sun wouldn't set for another two hours. Surely, Cash would arrange those fireworks before dark. Would he enlist the boys' help or keep it a surprise?

His comment that he'd blown up much bigger things before served only to remind her of his return to combat and dangerous missions. As part of the 2nd Marine Raider Battalion, Cash was assigned places others couldn't or wouldn't go. She'd never liked the idea of him in harm's way. She respected it, sure. She respected him even more for doing what many couldn't, but it didn't sit well and never would.

"Come on, boys, I have a job that I need your help with." Cash walked around and handed her the sturdy bow rake. "I'll take them out front to set up in the driveway. Keep an eye on the fire."

Monica saluted. He might have an air of authority, but she knew the gentleness inside the hard exterior.

"Cute."

She wanted to tell him that he was even *cuter*, but held her tongue. Flirting with him wasn't wise. Neither was falling in love with him. Watching him walk away with the boys, she promised herself she'd find a way to rein those feelings back in, because she had to.

After staring into the flames for another ten minutes or so, she noticed the enormous fire had burned down some. It was still hot, but she could get close enough to push stray bits of branches and sticks up into the flames, banking the blaze and exposing a ring of scorched earth around the burning mound.

She stepped back, rested her elbow on the rake handle and waited for more of the limbs to burn down. She could just barely hear the voices of Cash and the boys. How long did it take to set up a few fireworks?

Again, Monica walked around the burning pile, pushing sticks and burned branches into it and then watching it burn back down. Working the pile had a calming effect, but her mind still raced. What would chemotherapy do to her? A necessary evil, and yet would she fully recover from it or would there be lingering side effects that cropped up later in life? Namely, the inability to conceive. What else might there be?

After another half hour or more, the mound was considerably smaller than when they'd started. She'd worked up a sweat along with a bad case of dread. She really didn't want to do the whole cancer treatment thing, but there was no escaping it. Not for her.

At the sound of the slider opening and closing, Monica turned. Cash exited the cabin with a tray cluttered with pop cans, mustard, hot dogs and buns. Ethan followed with a chair, and behind him, Owen carried the bag of marshmallows.

Monica laid the rake down and dashed toward the little firepit in the yard to grab a couple more chairs. She needed to get her head back to simple pleasures, for now. "More hot dogs?"

Cash grinned. "I'm hungry."

She set the chairs down and went for the last one, but Cash stalled her.

"I'll get it. Roast me a hot dog?" He gave her begging puppy eyes. "Please."

She couldn't refuse that look. "Will do if you bring back the skewers from the firepit."

She watched as he walked beyond the firepit and entered the pole barn.

Monica waited for him to return. "Didn't you bring the long skewers with you?"

"Something even better." From under his arm, he handed over the long handle of a campfire basket. She could roast a whole bunch of hot dogs. "Found it on the shelf. You might want to sterilize it in the flames."

She rolled her eyes. Of course she would.

"I'm going to take Owen to find some long sticks," Ethan said, standing a little taller.

"Okay." Monica shared a look with Cash, who settled

into the campfire chair he'd fetched along with a little stand for the tray.

He grabbed a soft drink can and opened the top. "Want one?"

She reached for the can and their fingers overlapped. It shouldn't have been a big deal, but she might as well have touched a live wire from the way her arm tingled.

Cash must have felt it, too, because he grabbed her wrist when she pulled away, causing pop to splash onto her thumb.

"Please stop." Her voice came out low and raspy.

He let go, raising his hands in surrender. "Stop what?"

"You know what, and it won't work."

"I've been thinking about that—"

"How are these, Uncle Cash?" Ethan held up long, tender green branches still full of leaves.

Cash stepped away to help his nephew. "Those look pretty good."

Grateful for the interruption, Monica grabbed the wire grill basket and poked it into the flames. Since when had Cash been thinking about them getting involved? He was crazy, and also tempting her beyond reason.

She would be crazy to entertain a future together.

Until she was cured of cancer, she couldn't hold on to any hope for a life with this man, no matter how much she wanted one.

What was he doing? Cash was in no position to rethink anything. His circumstances hadn't changed. His desire to lead his men without worries back home remained. Yet, deep down, he wanted a life with Monica. A bigger one than he had. He wanted to play their own game of life, ending up with a pink peg followed by a blue.

Maybe he always had. There. He'd finally admitted it. Didn't mean he would act on it. Monica had been pretty clear about not wanting to be the wife of a marine. He glanced at her and admired the way she'd pulled her long ponytail into a messy bun at the top of her head. Some of the strands fell in wisps around her face. His gut twisted. Maybe she was right. It wouldn't work and they shouldn't even try. There were too many risks.

Sitting around the fire waiting for it to get dark enough to light the fireworks out front, Cash polished off the last bite of his hot dog. He glanced at the boys, leaning back in their camp chairs. Both had smears of marshmallow all over their mouths. Their faces were dirty, too. Owen sported a soot streak that ran the length of his cheek.

"When are we going to shoot off the fireworks?" Ethan asked for the third time.

"Soon, buddy. The sun just set. Let's give it a few minutes to get darker or else it's not as good." Cash stretched his legs toward the dwindling fire.

Monica kept up with raking the burned limbs into the fire, decreasing its size. They'd all inched their chairs closer to feel the heat and of course roast more marsh-mallows.

"Their mom comes tomorrow, right?" Monica held up the nearly empty bag of marshmallows.

Cash nodded. "Along with their grandma, my mom. Why?"

Monica smirked. "They ate a lot of these."

"So?"

"So…look at them." Monica lowered her voice to a whisper. "I hope they don't get sick."

Cash chuckled at the sight. The boys sank low, as if they couldn't stuff another thing in their little bellies. "What's to get sick on? It's just air and—"

"Sugar," the two adults said in unison.

Only Monica sounded accusatory, as if he should know better. He didn't. What kind of father would he make when he looked forward to the next big thrill? Would having kids of his own dampen that? Would Monica? He'd never been a sit-at-home kind of guy and he didn't see that ever changing. Although having a family meant that would have to change.

"They'll be fine." Cash waved away her concern. If they got sick, then next time they might not wolf down so many marshmallows.

"A typical guy response, if ever I heard one." Monica snorted.

"That guy you were seeing, would he say something like that?" Cash wanted to know what kind of man had captured her interest.

Her eyes widened with surprise, and then narrowed. "Why do you ask?"

He shrugged. This annoying pinch of jealousy was a new sensation. And he didn't like it one bit, but he had to know.

Monica sighed. "He bailed before I could give an honest answer to that question. I knew him for years, even worked on community projects with him, but I guess I didn't really know him."

"His loss," Cash growled.

He didn't like the guy. He didn't like that the man had dumped her, either, but was glad she wasn't seeing him.

Cash hoped she never saw him again. The mere idea that they could eventually get back together turned Cash's stomach. Which was crazy, when he'd just decided he wouldn't pursue Monica himself.

He checked his watch. Eight forty-five was good enough, he supposed. He slapped his jean-clad knees and stood. "I think we should go out front and get started on those fireworks."

Both boys jumped up and darted around to the driveway in front of the cabin. They moved pretty well for overdoing it on marshmallows. He reached for the rake Monica held. "I can put that away."

She stared at the low flames. "Is it okay to leave it like this?"

"The ground is damp. It'll be okay, but I'll check it again before bed."

"Won't you need the rake?"

He looked at the large ring of dirt surrounding the now small mound. "That fire's not going anywhere but out."

If he could simply follow that advice when it came to Monica… He needed to let the fire inside him burn out, as well.

Monica headed for the back door of the cabin. "I need to get the sparklers and then I'll meet you in front."

"Okay." He put the rake away in the pole barn and shut the door. Walking around to the driveway, he found the boys standing over the canned fireworks he'd set up, looking down with a little too much interest.

"Ethan, Owen, come here." Cash knelt on one knee and lay a hand on each boy's shoulder. "Listen close. These are dangerous and I won't light any of them unless you stay back. You got it?"

They both nodded.

He wasn't so bad at being a dad, even if only for a while.

The boys dashed toward the deck, where Monica held up a box of sparklers. "I thought we could light these while we wait for it to get a little darker."

"Good idea. Keep them on the deck, though." He grabbed the box of long matches that he'd left on top of his car.

He watched as the three of them waved the sparklers around and dipped and twirled. Monica laughed as she waved hers high in the air.

With the last bit of dusty rose color from the sunset in the background and the sparks flying around her head, she very much looked like the storybook princess the boys thought she was when they'd first arrived.

A lot had happened since then. In four days, he'd reconnected with Monica on a deeper level. They weren't kids anymore and that's what made being around her so tricky. He'd always cared for her, but he'd never let it go beyond that. Until now.

Monica stashed the last burned-out sparkler stick back in the box and then took a seat on the edge of the deck, the boys on either side of her. With an arm around each of them, she called out, "We're ready when you are."

Cash wasn't ready for the feelings coursing through his veins and pumping out of his heart. He wasn't ready for all those color combinations he'd drawn with crayons, as a conduit for more feelings he hadn't been ready to face. Hadn't wanted to face.

"Here we go." He lit the match and touched it to the

first couple of Roman candles and then stepped back to watch the streak of light and color.

Monica and the boys clapped.

He bowed, accepting their praise, but he was only getting started. He'd purchased quite a few fireworks here in Michigan that were illegal in North Carolina. He lit two more canisters and stepped back.

Both caught at the same time and launched into the sky to explode with green and purple lights and rat-a-tap-tap firing sounds.

This time he heard sincerely captivated sounding oohs and ahhs from the front deck. He'd impressed not only the boys, but Monica, too.

He went down the line he'd set up, lighting, then stepping back as each firecracker soared into the air and exploded in a shower of sparks and booms.

Owen held his ears at the last round and leaned into Monica.

Cash had saved the biggest and loudest for the end. Maybe he should have purchased tamer options, but the look on Ethan's face made it worth the noise. The kid was in total awe.

"Thanks, Uncle Cash."

Cash stepped closer to the deck. "Had to do something special for our last night."

"Are you leaving?" Ethan looked confused.

"Nope. But Monica has to go tomorrow morning after the driveway is cleared." He glanced at her.

He wished he hadn't because she looked sad, and he didn't like seeing Monica sad.

"Do you have to?" Ethan whined.

"I have to get home to my job," Monica's voice was soft and sweet and loaded with regret.

"Why?" Owen's voice squeaked.

Monica flashed him a quick look of surprise before gently cupping the five-year-old's chin. "What did you say?"

"Why do you have to go when you don't want to?"

That was clear as a bell. Cash knelt before Owen. "You talked!"

Owen nodded.

Ethan cheered.

Monica laughed, but tears welled up in her eyes as she looked into the little boy's face. "I have to go, Owen. I have things I need to do back home. Important things."

The boy still looked confused. Obviously, work wasn't a good enough excuse for a five-year-old.

Cash gathered them all into his arms for a group hug and whispered a quick prayer of gratitude. "Thank You, God."

Monica responded with a watery sounding, "Amen."

Resting his forehead against hers while they embraced the boys, he wondered why Owen had said that Monica didn't want to leave. To him, she'd seemed pretty anxious to go, so why didn't she tell the kid he was way off?

Monica watched as Cash lifted Owen and tossed him high in the air, only to catch the giggling five-year-old, who egged him on to do it again and again. He talked like he'd never stopped. Like his silence hadn't been a big deal.

"Let's call your mom." Cash looked beyond relieved.

She knew this was one less thing he had to worry about after he left. She didn't want to replace it with added concerns over her.

He ushered the boys inside, then turned to hold the door for her. "Coming in?"

She shook her head. "I'm going to hang out here and check the fire. I'll be in in a bit."

He searched her eyes.

She smiled and waved him away. "Call their mom."

Once the door was closed, Monica got up and headed for the backyard and the fire they'd left there. It was nothing but glowing embers now. She grabbed a camp chair and sat down close enough to feel the warmth from it, but the reality of the coming weeks chilled her to the bone.

Tipping her head back, she gazed up at the moon peeking through breaks in the clouds. Not a good night for stargazing, but a quiet night now that the fireworks were over.

They had to be over between her and Cash, too. Tomorrow, she'd leave, and that would be that. Back to their own lives, and this weekend would simply be another cherished memory.

"Thank You, Lord, for bringing Owen's speech back," she whispered into the darkness.

God answers prayer.

She knew that, but could she rest assured that her prayers for healing would also be answered? She didn't want to go through any of what waited ahead, and yet what choice did she have?

"Hey." Cash touched her shoulder.

Monica looked up. "I didn't even hear you come out."

"You were deep in thought." Cash gestured toward the cabin. "The boys are getting ready for bed, but they want you to tuck them in."

Monica swallowed hard. A lump of emotion seemed

stuck there ever since Owen had spoken. The little guy knew she didn't want to leave. These past few days concentrating on his issues had worked wonders on getting her mind off her own.

She stared at Cash's offered hand and took it, enjoying the feeling of his strength and the warmth of his skin. She didn't let go as they made their way back to the cabin, glad he didn't say anything. He didn't ask anything, either. He simply held her hand, stroking the back of it with his thumb.

When they stepped inside, she could see the boys were already in the bunk beds.

"You guys washed your face and hands?" Cash asked.

"Yes," they answered together.

The boys hadn't washed up very well and Monica chuckled at the blackened and sticky looking streak of marshmallow across Owen's cheek.

"Let's say our prayers." Cash held Ethan's hand and reached out his other hand to her.

She took it and scooped up Owen's little hand in turn. There was dirt on his wrist.

"Dear Lord," Cash started. "Give us a good night's sleep and protect their mom and grandma's travel here. And keep Monica safe and well as she heads home. Amen."

Monica let go and leaned toward Ethan. "I might be gone before you wake up, so take care, okay?"

"Okay." He gave her a hug.

She bent to give Owen a hug, too.

"Why are you sad?" The little guy could read her like a book, and now that he talked, it wasn't cool. Good thing she was leaving before the little tyke uncovered more of her secrets.

Monica cleared her throat. "Because I'm going to miss you guys. This has been a lot of fun."

Owen nodded, seemingly satisfied, and gave her a big hug.

"Sleep tight." She gave him a squeeze before letting go and exiting the room.

Cash followed her out, leaving the door slightly ajar as usual.

"I should probably turn in, too. Early morning and all."

Cash looked through her. "Yeah."

She couldn't move.

"When are you going to tell me what's wrong?" His voice was low and coaxing.

Monica rolled her eyes, feeling them fill with tears. "I don't want to."

He stepped close and wrapped his arms around her waist, pulling her close. "Why?"

Monica held on tight, resting her head against his. "Because."

He scooped her up in one swift movement.

"Cash!" She pushed at the solid wall of his chest, but he only held on tighter as he carried her to the couch.

Monica chuckled when he set her down. "I can't believe you can carry me. I'm no lightweight."

He brushed away one of the tears that had spilled over to run down her cheek. "I've lifted heavier."

"Really?" Monica squeaked.

He laughed then. "No."

She punched his shoulder. "Thanks a lot."

"I'm teasing you." His gaze turned serious. "What if I told you that I'm going to miss you? I want to see you again when I'm on leave."

Her eyes widened. "Don't say that."

"Why not?"

She scrambled to the far corner of the couch. "Because…"

"Because why?" His eyes narrowed as if putting puzzle pieces together and not liking the picture one bit. "This guy you broke up with. You're not thinking of getting back with him or anything, are you?"

"No!" Monica gasped, then shook her head. She had to laugh, actually. "No."

"Good, because I'd have turned him inside out if you had said yes." His dark gray eyes looked even darker. The sight was pretty intimidating.

She had a feeling that Cash would be a far worse force to contend with than her brothers. More protective even than her father. Brady wouldn't have stood a chance. Next to Cash, what did she ever see in Brady, anyway?

"I told you we weren't serious."

What would Cash think if she told him there hadn't been anyone serious in her life? Not that she hadn't tried, but he'd always been there, lurking in the shadows of her heart. Part of her had always hoped that someday they'd—

She stood. "It's late. I'm going to bed."

He reached for her hand and yanked her back down next to him. "Kiss me good-night."

The man played with fire.

"Just one." Monica leaned close, planting her lips on his.

The kiss they shared was quick and hard and over much too soon, so she kissed him again. Evidently, she liked playing with fire, too, and if she didn't want to get burned to a crisp, she'd better end it now.

Pulling back, she scrunched her face. "Sorry."

He gave her a grim smile. "I'm not."

"You should be. We don't have a future."

"Why? And tell me the truth this time."

Monica sat back and weighed the cost of telling him. On the one hand, he might find out eventually from Matthew. She knew they still kept in touch. On the other, if he backed away like Brady had, then she'd have her confirmation that they were never meant to be. That'd be safer for both of them, wouldn't it?

She took a deep breath and hoped she did the right thing. "I have cancer, Cash. Thursday's appointment is with a team of doctors to choose which path to best combat it."

She watched his face fall, and then fear crept into his eyes—cold and distant. Right before her, he closed up shop and shuttered his soul from view.

With a sick feeling, she knew she'd just chased Cash Miller away for good.

Chapter Twelve

Cash sat back in an attempt to shield himself from the emotional grenade she'd just launched, but it blew up and took him down. The nastiest of words, *cancer* reverberated through him over and over. His stomach felt as if it had dropped to his feet as the realization of what she'd just told him sank in deep.

Anger bubbled up next. He may have cheated death, but it always came looking for him by taking the ones who meant the most to him. This time it threatened Monica. *His Monica.* He wasn't sure he had what it took to fight it. Like a coward, he wanted to run and never look back.

How bad—

"How bad?" His voice cracked.

"Stage two out of four." She shrugged, but her pretty blue eyes were filled with sympathy. She was the one who was sick, yet she felt sorry for him.

The news kicked him in the gut, followed by a numbing sensation that made him light-headed. He felt sorry for himself, too. He didn't want to think about her suffering in any way. Yet she would. She'd be poked and prodded. He clenched and unclenched his fists.

"Monica, I'm so sorry," he finally choked out.

She gave him a brave smile. "Bad timing, huh? See, we're not meant to be. Maybe not ever. I can't stand the thought of you over there getting blown up, and I sure don't want you saddled with my issues. Who knows how long this might last."

It felt like a punch of reality in the face. One he understood all too well. Neither one of them could guarantee they'd be around in the next five years. He didn't know much about cancer, but he knew it could kill. Just like he could get killed.

He just sat there, staring ahead, dazed.

She did, too.

She'd finally trusted him with the truth of what was going on with her, and now that he knew, he wished he didn't. Almost.

He wrapped his arms around her and pulled her close, stretching out his leg so she could lean into him. He only held her, glad that she didn't push him away. In fact, Monica sank into him, holding on just as tightly.

He didn't know how long they stayed that way, but long enough for his leg to fall asleep. Evidently, Monica did, too. Her long, lithe body had gone limp against him a few minutes ago.

He nudged her and whispered, "Monica."

She pulled back and blinked her eyes, trying to focus. "Sorry."

He chucked her chin and murmured, "Go to bed, baby. I'll see you in the morning."

"Good night, Cash." She slipped from the couch and silently climbed the steps to the loft.

He remained where he was. Frozen yet burning with renewed anger at God. Why did He have to take everyone away from him? Everyone who mattered?

Cash wanted to holler and break things, but destroying this cabin would do nothing to change what he'd heard. Besides, it'd wake up the boys. And Matthew would never speak to him again if he trashed his uncle's cabin.

Monica? She'd understand. She'd always understood too much.

He stood up and put weight on his leg in an attempt to shake the needles out of it. Grabbing the throw blankets from the other night, Cash lay back down on the couch. Plumping up the pillows, he covered himself. He'd sleep here tonight, in case Monica needed him for some reason.

His sister-in-law had said her crew would arrive early to clear the driveway. Sleeping on the couch, he'd have a better chance of hearing them. Besides, he wasn't going to miss saying goodbye to Monica in the morning.

It dawned on him that they'd never really said *goodbye* before. In the past, they'd dance around it with a *see-ya-later* followed by a shove to the shoulder or tug of hair. It would be like Monica to slip out so they wouldn't have to say those final words. He'd ducked out two years ago at Matthew's wedding rather than have to say goodbye to Monica.

He wasn't going to miss this send-off. Sleeping on the couch, he'd wake up when she came down those stairs and he'd tell her—what? That he'd take her place if he could? He wasn't sure what he'd say to her. Nothing seemed adequate compared to what she faced in the coming months.

Cancer…

He slammed his fists against the couch, then closed his eyes and tried to pray. He didn't feel much like praying, but he started anyway.

Lord…

He stopped. He had no words other than one.

Why?

Monica woke up late. Really late, but then it had taken forever to fall back to sleep, between her own tossing and turning and listening to Cash's breathing from downstairs. She hadn't a clue why he'd slept on the couch, but she'd learned something new about Cash Miller— he snored.

Slipping down the loft stairs with her packed suitcase, she inhaled the luscious aromas of brewed coffee and something sweet-smelling baking in the oven. She remained quiet in case the boys were still sleeping.

"Monica!" Owen ran toward her and threw his arms around her legs.

"Let her get down the steps, Owen," Cash scolded.

The little guy backed up and waited.

Monica took the last two steps. She leaned her suitcase against the railing and hugged Owen. "Good morning." Then of Cash she asked, "The driveway got cleared, right?"

"First thing this morning, yes. Took them only an hour. My mom and sister-in-law will be here shortly. They're early. Want breakfast?"

She wanted to leave and fast, but her stomach had a mind of its own and rumbled orders to feed it.

Cash heard the gurgle. "I'll take that as a yes. Coffee?"

"Please." She grabbed the cream from the fridge and then slipped onto a stool at the island.

How could he act as if nothing had happened between them? As if he didn't know? She switched rails on that train of thought. This was far better than doom and gloom. Brady had acted offended when she'd told him, as if she were to blame somehow. Like she'd been outside without a coat and had caught a cold. She was glad he'd tossed her aside.

Cash had simply held her. He didn't hound her with questions, nor did he get mad. He simply offered her comfort, and she'd actually relaxed, feeling more secure than ever before. So much so that she'd fallen asleep in his arms.

Cash handed her a cup of steaming brew with a spoon and the dispenser of sugar.

"Thank you." She'd told him about the cancer because he needed to know why they couldn't be. He needed to stop rethinking his goal of remaining emotionally unfettered. Telling him had been the right thing for both of them.

Wasn't it?

"Welcome." His gazed rested on her for far too long.

She could feel it, so she looked up into his face and wished she hadn't. Despite his chipper chatter, his eyes were wild. He looked angry and full of concern and maybe even afraid. For as long as she'd known him, Cash Miller had never before shown her any fear.

She looked away. She was afraid enough; she didn't need to see it reflected back at her. "So, what's for breakfast? It smells amazing."

"French toast casserole. It's almost done."

She tried to act normal, like he did. "I'm impressed."

He shrugged. "It's easier than making it one slice at time. Same ingredients, just stuffed into a pan."

Owen climbed onto the chair next to her. "Ethan's talking to Mom."

"Oh?" She looked, and sure enough, Ethan exited the bedroom with Cash's phone in his hand.

"She wants to talk to you." The eight-year-old handed it to Cash before launching himself onto the other chair next to her.

"Yeah?" Cash gazed at her again as he talked to the boys' mom. "No, I don't think we need anything. We have plenty of milk. Yep. See you soon." He ended the call and pocketed the phone. "They're at the corner store on the main road. You'll get to meet Ruth."

"Appears so." She'd met Cash's mom on a couple occasions before—after Cash's father had died and then again at Cash's high school graduation, since it was the same as Matthew's.

"She'll want to thank you."

Monica tipped her head. "For what?"

"I told Ruth about the coloring and all that."

What *all* did he say? Monica gave him a pointed look.

"Nothing about anything else." He nodded toward Owen.

The boy drank his milk, but was listening to every word they said, while his brother fiddled with a fidget spinner.

Monica relaxed. It was better this way, saying goodbye to Cash with the boys and his family here. Less chance of falling apart.

The timer rang, announcing the French toast casserole was done, and Cash responded with precision and speed. Opening the oven door and using two pinecone-print mitts, he pulled the pan out and set it on the stovetop, followed by a smaller pan covered with foil.

"What can I do?" she asked, but knew the answer. He had everything under control like always.

"Not a thing." He then set syrup and butter and the gallon of milk on the island. "I'll serve it since it's hot."

"Sounds good." Monica watched him.

His biceps flexed where the short-sleeved T-shirt didn't fully cover his arm. Cash was cut from hours spent lifting and running, but then he was a soldier ready for action at a moment's notice.

She'd always hated thinking about what kind of *action* he might encounter next. Seeing that ugly scar above his belt hadn't helped. The image was permanently stamped into her mind.

He set a plate of layered French toast with three sausage links before her and winked. "There's more if you want it."

Her belly growled again, but her appetite was shriveling up and dying. "This should do it."

He served up slightly smaller portions to the boys before serving himself. They all sat at the island in a line as if they were at a diner, and Cash said a quick prayer.

"Amen!" Owen hollered, and dug in.

Ethan rolled his eyes and doused his plate in syrup.

Monica looked at Cash. It was as if a switch had been flipped. The younger kid talked as if he'd never been quiet.

Cash shrugged.

They ate in silence, the boys happily shoveling in the food while Monica forced herself to eat, and Cash ate normally. After a few minutes, they heard a knock at the front door.

Both boys ran for it, pushing and shoving each other.

Monica stood as the two Miller women arrived. Polishing off her last bite, she took her plate to the sink, while the Miller boys gave respective hugs and welcomes.

"You must be Monica." Cash's sister-in-law held out her hand. "I'm Ruth."

Monica smiled at the pretty woman with golden eyes before her and grasped her hand for a firm shake. Now she knew where the boys got their red hair. "Nice to meet you."

"Thank you for everything you did for my boys. Cash told me how Owen took to you, and, well…" Her eyes grew watery. "I can't thank you enough."

Monica's own throat grew thick, but she swallowed hard. She was far too emotional these days. "I enjoyed time with them and I really needed this."

That was indeed true. This past weekend had been not only fun, but good for keeping her mind off her up-coming appointment. Off her diagnosis. She'd have been miserable here all alone. "Well, I'd best get going. I have work piling up for me back home."

Ruth surprised her by reaching out for a hug. "Safe travels. I hope to see you again soon."

"Thanks." Monica returned the woman's embrace and then turned to greet Cash's mom. "How are you, Mrs. Miller?"

"Doing well. Nice to see you again, dear Monica. Give your parents my best."

"I will." Next came the boys. They gave her quick

hugs, as they were distracted by what their grandmother had brought them. So Monica took the chance to make her escape.

"I'll walk you out," Cash said quietly, as he hoisted her small suitcase as if it were light as a book.

Monica grabbed her empty cooler and braced herself for telling him goodbye. "Let's not drag this out."

He chuckled, but kept walking to her car, where he lifted the rear hatch and tossed in her bag, then waited for her to nestle the cooler next to it.

She opened her driver's side door as he shut the back. Needing to put some distance between them, she stood beside her car.

He closed that distance. Reaching up behind her neck, he gripped the back of her head and gazed into her eyes. "Take care."

Her heart beat so hard that she thought maybe he'd hear it, like he'd heard her stomach growls. She didn't want him to kiss her, but desperately wanted him to in the same panicked thought.

With one quick glance toward the cabin, she spotted his family looking on. They quickly dashed away from the big windows. "They see us."

"I don't care."

"I do."

"Monica, Monica, Monica," he teased. "Some things never change."

Like going their separate ways again.

"Some things never change," she repeated.

Sliding his other hand around her waist, he drew her close for a simple hug.

Only it wasn't simple.

Her eyes closed and her breath caught and she wrapped her arms around his shoulders. "Bye."

He tucked his face against her neck and briefly kissed her throat, then gave her a quick squeeze and let go. "Goodbye, Monica."

Wobbly in the knees from hearing him say the one word they'd never said before, she managed to get into the driver's seat and start the engine.

He closed her door and stepped back.

With one last look and brief wave, she backed up and headed for home.

"You're awfully quiet this evening," Ruth said, as she dried a dish and put it away.

He'd washed the dishes and stacked them in the drainer.

Cash shrugged and walked away from the kitchen. "Not much to say."

His mom took the honors of tucking the boys into bed tonight by reading them a story. One with giants and princesses, and he felt the pain of Monica's leaving all over again.

His sister-in-law nodded toward them. "The boys want to know if Monica is your girlfriend."

"They could have asked me, and the answer would have been no." He frowned, not liking that reply. Not liking that they'd parted the way they had, saying *goodbye*.

Ruth smiled. "I don't think they thought about it until after she left because you've worn a long face ever since."

He might as well have been run over by a tank, he thought, and mumbled an unintelligible response.

"You're in love with her." Ruth gave him a pity-filled smile. "I can tell."

He shrugged, but didn't answer. He hadn't admitted that to anyone, let alone himself. Everyone he loved most died. He didn't want to love Monica, only to see her fade away and die. If he refused to love her, maybe she'd live… He cringed. That was something his nephews might think.

After a long silence, he finally said, "She has cancer."

"So?"

"So?" Cash looked at his brother's wife like it should be obvious.

It wasn't to Ruth.

She set the dish towel down with a fierceness he rarely saw. "Two weeks ago, if you had asked me if I would have married Cole knowing he would die too soon, leaving our boys without a father, I might have said no. The pain was too fresh, but now… It wouldn't have mattered had he died days after our honeymoon, I would still have married him. Over and over, I would have."

He looked at her hard. "Why?"

"Because any time spent with your brother was worth it. I was blessed with eleven years that were the best of my life. I wouldn't trade them for anything, nor would I have given them up simply because they'd be cut short and the pain is more than I ever thought possible."

Cash didn't want any more pain. He'd suffered enough losses, might yet suffer still. He didn't want to build a life with Monica only to lose her too soon. He didn't want to go through what his sister-in-law described.

"Maybe I can't make that trade," he finally said.

His sister-in-law touched his forearm, looking mournful. "I'm sorry about that."

"Me, too." He headed toward the glass slider leading to the backyard. "I'm going to get some air."

She nodded.

He ducked into the boys' room first. His mom had moved on to reading *The Jungle Book,* and Ethan was already out cold, but Owen listened with wide eyes.

"Good night, buddy." He kept his voice low.

"Night, Uncle Cash." Owen hadn't bothered to whisper.

Cash glanced at Ethan, who snorted, rolled over and went on sleeping. He shared an amused look with his mom before slipping outside the door into the darkness.

Glancing at the stars above, he hated that his nephews would always be affected by the loss of their dad. Cash had never gotten over his own father's death. He walked around with a hole still inside him. Cole had understood that, too, since he carried the same sensation. The same loss. It was a hole those two boys would now experience.

Last time Cash checked, that hole had widened when Cole died, but it would swallow him up if Monica didn't make it. He didn't even know what kind of cancer she had. Monica hadn't said. He hadn't asked, either, not sure he wanted to know.

He was a coward and no better than that loser who'd dumped her. Had he walked because of the cancer?

Cash scoured the property, making sure everything had been put back in its place. Passing by the circle of ashes that was once their huge limb pile, he recalled Monica standing in the tall grass. That image of her seemed so clear. He remembered her standing with one hand resting on the rake and the other on her hip. She had that crooked grin on her face. The one she used after mocking him for something.

He missed her.

Slipping into the camp chair still sitting by the ring of ashes, he bowed his head between his hands.

"God…" He didn't know what to pray.

He'd prayed for help with the boys a few days ago and God had answered by sending Monica. Why did He do that, only to take her away again?

You let her go, idiot!

Cash groaned, but he wasn't done with God. This was His fault, too. Why had He let Monica get cancer? Why had He let Cole die? Too many questions without answers. It always came back to that.

"God, you know how I'm feeling. I'm mad as—" He stopped.

Hadn't he told the boys that God understood exactly how they felt? God had given His only son to die on the cross so that all who believed in Him might live.

Cash considered those crayons he'd used that night and how coloring had released something deep inside him. Maybe he should try that again and see if it helped him sort through some of this. He knew fear well, but he'd never been this afraid before.

Could he stop shutting down and instead open himself up enough to be there for Monica, even if it hurt worse than anything he'd experienced thus far? Even if it meant he'd lose her in the end?

Cash closed his eyes. He was a marine and marines didn't leave their brothers in arms to face a battle alone. He could provide Monica with moral support at the very least. Show that he cared for her more than protecting himself.

That's the way he faced every mission.

Maybe it was time to face a new mission in his life no matter how long or short it might be. God had answered his prayer by bringing Monica to the cabin, and God had kept her there until Owen had talked.

Maybe there was more to her staying than just for the boys. Maybe God knew that Cash needed to talk, as well, but in a language only the heart understood.

Chapter Thirteen

Monica sat in her office and stared at the computer screen. Her assistant had left long ago. It was late, after seven in the evening, and she still couldn't get this web design right. She worked out of her garage, which had been converted into an office space complete with a bathroom and coffee bar area. For clients, of course.

Not that many met her here. She typically went to their place of business so she could get a feel for what they did, then nail their branding and online presence. Her own business branding could use a face-lift. The name Website Design and Marketing by Monica seemed pretty generic. Specific, yes, but boring.

She slumped in her chair and sighed. She'd been home two full days. Tonight would be her second night spent alone like always. Only alone didn't feel right anymore. She missed Cash. She missed him something awful.

After rubbing her eyes, she dropped her head in her hands.

"I thought I'd find you out here."

Her mom's voice brought her head up fast. "Hi."

Too late. Her mother had seen her anguish, and her

mom's brow furrowed accordingly. "Don't push yourself too hard."

"I'm not. Just trying to catch up." And keep her mind busy.

"Monica, it's going to be okay. Tomorrow's appointment with the oncology team will answer a lot of our questions."

"Thanks, Mom." Monica nodded.

Oh, how she wished this was one of those times where her mother could put a cartoon bandage over everything and make it all better.

Her mom planned to go with her, and that was a good thing, since Monica was terrified after all the researching she'd done online. She really didn't know what direction to take. Go aggressive or play it conservative. She knew her mom well enough to know that she'd opt for the least invasive and painful choice, but that might not be the right one in the long run.

Helen Zelinsky stepped closer and brushed Monica's hair behind her ear. "Have you eaten dinner?"

Monica scrunched her nose to keep from falling apart at the waver in her mother's soft voice. "Not really hungry."

"That's it. You're coming with us."

"Us?"

"Your father and me. He's in the car. We were going out to dinner and I saw your office lights on. Your house is dark, Monica."

"The sun hasn't even set yet, so why would I turn on lights in the house?"

"You look like you could use a steak." Her mom completely changed the subject on her.

Monica laughed, but there was no real amusement in

it. If ever she sounded as hollow as she felt, it was now. Tomorrow's appointment would lay the groundwork for her cancer battle ahead. A fight she'd never wanted. A battle that could last a lifetime.

She stood and gave her mom a kiss on the cheek. "I won't be good company and I'm thinking of turning in early. Thanks for stopping, though. Tell Dad some other time."

Her mother looked disappointed and concerned, but gave her a big hug.

Monica held on tight.

When her mother stepped back, she gave Monica a hard look. "You sure you're okay? I can stay. Your father and I can come back after dinner. Maybe you should come home with us tonight."

Monica shook her head. "Thanks, but I have a few more sites to look into, and like you said, it's going to be fine. God's got this, right?"

Her mother wasn't convinced by her cavalier tone. She looked worried. "Maybe you should call Cash."

Monica glanced up sharply. "Why would you say that?"

That wise gaze didn't miss much. "Because you're thinking about him, aren't you?"

Of course she was, but she didn't want to admit it. She and Cash had agreed that they couldn't work. Not now. Probably not ever. They'd finally said the word *goodbye*.

"Does he know?" her mom asked.

Monica clenched her hands into fists, only to release them and wipe her palms against the backside of her shorts. "Yes. I told him."

"And?"

Man number two that she'd chased away. "Mom,

we're friends. Friends who've always gone in different directions."

Her mother squeezed her hand and looked right through her. "Call me if you need me. I don't care how late it is."

"I will. I promise." Monica squeezed back and walked her to the door. She waved at her dad, seated in the car waiting.

He honked the horn.

After she watched her parents drive out of sight, Monica saved her work and shut down the computer. She flicked off the light, shut and locked the door and headed for her house. Funny, but she never locked the doors to her home until she went to bed. Her office was locked any time she wasn't in it.

After entering the little bungalow situated two blocks from Main Street in Maple Springs, Michigan, Monica headed for her bedroom. She changed into a summery set of pajamas her mom had given her for her birthday a couple weeks ago.

Her gaze snagged on the beautiful crystal stork on her dresser. Cash had given it to her for her eighteenth birthday. It was a good twelve inches high and had most likely cost him a few bucks even back then. She still had the padded box that it came in.

Running her fingertips over the cool crystal, she then touched her lips, remembering the kisses they'd shared. Their first had been the night he'd given her the statue. Monica had been young and eager to kiss Cash in an attempt to purge the crush she'd had on him.

How wrong she'd been. Maybe it had been then that she'd realized she loved him. Had he asked her to go with him back then, she might have. But he didn't ask.

He hadn't asked this time, either. This time they'd cut those ties for good, finally putting words to what they'd always known. They had no future together. They'd never really had one other than in her foolish daydreams and wishes.

She closed her eyes as the image of that scar tearing up his middle burned through her thoughts. What other injuries awaited him? She'd never been able to watch those war movies her brothers liked, because the thought of Cash getting torn up in battle as portrayed on screen made her sick.

She touched the crystal stork again, letting the tears fall. "Oh, Cash, please be safe."

Cash packed the last of his bags and personal belongings from the small apartment over the garage of his brother's place. It wasn't much more than a room and a bathroom, but it's where he'd stayed when home on leave after his mother had sold her house and moved in with Cole and Ruth.

Even though he'd been here for nearly a month, he didn't have much. Just a couple duffels and a box of memorabilia Ruth wanted him to have from when he and Cole were kids.

Memories.

He'd made some with Monica over the years. Quite a few this past weekend. He wanted to make more. He ran his hand through his hair, then down his face, scratching the whiskers of his close beard. Even though the cabin had been full with his mom, Ruth and the boys, Cash hadn't been prepared for the emptiness that consumed him after Monica had left. He couldn't stay there with memories and images of her popping up all around. He didn't want to.

Once he'd made the decision to leave the Zelinsky cabin, his sister-in-law and mom followed suit. They didn't want to stay there in the woods without him, so they packed up, cleaned up and returned.

Now, he suffered from a serious case of cold feet in his plan to stop in Maple Springs before heading for Camp Lejeune. Tomorrow morning he'd leave before dawn and make it in time to hopefully convince Monica to let him join her for her afternoon doctor's appointment.

What if she didn't want him there? Worse, what if she didn't really want *him*? He'd find out soon enough.

Cash checked his watch, grabbed his phone and hit his contact for Matthew Zelinsky. Monica's brother might be on break about now as first mate on a Great Lakes freighter. Cash waited for his lifelong buddy to pick up. He'd rather not leave a message, but would if he had to. He wanted Matthew's approval before carrying out this new mission.

"Cash, what's up?"

He blew out his breath. "Hey. You busy?"

"I have a few minutes. Everything okay?"

"I'm in love with your sister." There, he'd said it out loud. He heard suppressed laughter on the other end. "It's not funny."

"Sorry, but yeah, so?"

"So…" Cash wanted to growl into the phone. "I wanted you to know, and make sure you're okay with it."

"I've pretty much known for years. 'Bout time you're doing something about it."

Silence.

Cash wasn't sure yet what he was going to do. All

he knew was that he couldn't let Monica take this walk through cancer alone. He had to support her. He'd cheer her on from the sidelines, through constant contact. He wanted her to beat this and then—

"You are going to do something about it, right?"

"Yeah."

Again, Matthew laughed. "Don't sound so bummed. Monica's a great girl."

"I know she is. I also know about the cancer, Matty, and I can't just walk away." He couldn't be like that other guy. The loser who had dumped her.

"I'm glad you're not." Matthew sounded somber, but relieved. "Godspeed, buddy."

"Thanks." Cash disconnected and took another deep breath.

This wasn't going to be easy. In fact, this might be the hardest thing he'd ever done. He'd offer his heart knowing it could get broken in two depending on what that doctor had to say.

Cash closed his eyes, recounting what Ruth had said about her years with Cole being the best of her life. Whatever time he had with Monica would be worth it. He'd make it that way.

He carried his stuff downstairs and loaded it in his car, leaving behind only what he'd need in the morning. With that done, he entered the main house, where he spotted his sister-in-law through the kitchen window. The sun hadn't set yet, but his nephews started school the following week. Ruth liked them on a regular schedule, so he was pretty sure they'd be soon heading for bed.

His sister-in-law was at the sink, unloading the dishwasher. "Hey. Are you ready to go?"

"Car's packed. I thought I'd say goodbye tonight,

since I'm heading out so early tomorrow. Where are the boys?"

Ruth nodded toward the family room. "Watching TV with your mom."

Cash turned to go, but Ruth stalled him.

"Thanks for everything you did for the boys. They loved going to that cabin with you."

Cash nodded. "It went pretty well."

His sister-in-law handed him a small gift bag. "I have a little something for you to take to Monica. You know, as a thank-you."

He glanced inside. "What is it?"

"Some ginger candies, a notebook with a pen and a thank-you card, of course."

Cash pulled out the small sparkly notebook with matching pen and knew Monica would love it. Lifting the ginger candies, he felt his stomach turn at the small print on the bag that stated these were good for nausea.

He couldn't stand the thought of Monica getting sick and suffering through treatment. He hated even more that he wouldn't be right there with her.

Ruth touched his arm. "I've heard they really do help."

"Thanks." His voice came out sounding thick, so he didn't say more.

Searching out his mom and nephews in the family room, Cash took a seat and finished watching a Disney movie with them. He tried to focus on the story, but his mind wandered. He'd never wanted worries back home that might impede his judgment in the field. Could he manage to keep it together over the course of training for the next mission?

The way he looked at it, the only way he'd find any

kind of peace before he left was to know exactly what Monica was up against. The good and the bad. Whether she wanted his love or even returned it, he needed her to know that he was sticking by her. They were in this fight together.

Thursday morning, Monica lay in bed staring at the ceiling while sun streamed in along the sides of her Roman shades. The air was warm, with mild temperatures overnight promising to climb during the day. A last blast of summer heat before the kids started school next week.

She didn't care about getting up and going to her office. Not today. She didn't care about getting work done, either. Couldn't focus on it anyway.

She'd typed a bunch of questions on her tablet based on what she'd found online. None of it had given her any hope, in fact quite the opposite. She'd read one too many stories of women who'd battled breast cancer for years. Several had gone into remission, only to one day find that the cancer had crept back into their lives. Monica didn't want anything to ever creep back in on her. Which meant hitting this disease aggressively.

What would Cash think about it all? What advice would he give?

She'd never told him what kind of cancer she had. Never explained what was at stake. The fear in his eyes had been enough for her to keep that to herself. She could possibly have reconstructive surgery, but she would never be the same.

Rolling onto her stomach, Monica buried her face deep in the pillow and screamed. It didn't make her feel any better.

Nothing did.

Flipping onto her back, she pounded the bed with her fists. "Why, God? Why me, why now?"

Nothing.

She quieted her thoughts and listened. Hard.

Still nothing.

God doesn't always answer right away, but He always answers on time.

It was something her mother had once said to her when she was young. Monica couldn't remember when or under what circumstances, but it came to her now. God knew her heart. He knew her fears as well as her desires, yet He required her trust.

God answers prayer.

She knew that. Had always known that, but this was where the rubber met the road, testing what she really believed. Could she truly act on her faith and trust the Lord with her body, her heart, her entire life? That was the tough part, even when things were good, but when things were bad, could she let go and simply trust in the Lord?

Dragging herself out of bed, Monica shuffled to the kitchen, made coffee and sulked. Not even the luscious smell of the freshly brewed special blend brought her any pleasure. She had every question she could imagine outlined on her tablet, but she still didn't feel ready.

Not at all.

After filling her cup and mixing in cream and sugar, Monica slumped on the couch. Staring out the window, she sipped her coffee. Her neighbor across the street was trimming the bushes around her small yard. A group of kids were heading to the beach early in anticipation of a hot day and a crowd. None of them had a clue. Life could change in an instant.

Closing her eyes, she knew she'd go stir-crazy waiting around all morning for her mom to pick her up after lunch. She downed the last of her coffee, changed into a pair of capri-length leggings and a long sport tank. After slipping into running shoes and pulling her hair into a ponytail, Monica grabbed her phone and earbuds and headed outside.

She didn't even bother stretching and took off down the block at a moderate jog. It had been at least a week since the last time she'd gone for a run. The morning was warm and it didn't take long to work up a sweat. She ignored the green light on her phone reminding her of messages waiting to be answered, cranked up the volume for the music stored on it, and upped her pace.

After twenty minutes, her muscles strained but responded well enough. She'd feel it the next morning, but she didn't care. She pounded the pavement, running faster than normal until it hurt. She finally stopped and bent over, breathing hard at the sharp stitch in her side.

She'd made it to the bluffs overlooking town and the street where Cash had lived growing up. She walked toward his old house with the big square porch. She'd been to the Miller house only once, after Mr. Miller had died. Monica had come with her mom to drop off a meal.

She'd never forget standing in the foyer while her mother took the food to the kitchen, and hearing Cash in the living room. She had moved forward to go in and offer her sympathy, but heard a girl's giggle and froze.

Cash hadn't been alone.

Backing into the wall as if she could disappear into the floral wallpaper there, she'd nearly died when he came around the corner and saw her. Her face had been scorching hot with embarrassment. He'd seemed a little awkward, as well, now that she thought about it.

Cash had looked uncomfortable, even sorry to see her, but he'd greeted her, calling her Stork before accusing her of lurking in the hallway. Fortunately, her mom was ready to go by then, so she didn't have to linger any longer.

Monica still didn't know who that girl might have been. It didn't matter. He was as out of reach now as he'd been back then.

Blowing out a breath, Monica turned away and headed home. No more thinking about Cash. He was gone and she'd be wise to let him go. From her thoughts and her heart.

She walked the several blocks back to her little house on the other side of town. Her thoughts continually strayed into dangerous territory as she remembered every detail of the time spent with Cash at her uncle's cabin. She even missed Ethan and Owen, and wished she'd had the forethought to get Ruth's phone number. She would have liked to call them, just to see how they were.

Rounding the last block, Monica stopped when she saw the black Dodge in her driveway. Her stomach dropped to the soles of her running shoes and her heart bounced around inside her chest. Hope mixed with a good dose of panic and irritation as she watched Cash knocking on her front door. She seriously considered turning around and running the opposite direction, but then he saw her.

Too late. She was caught.

Different from the time she'd just remembered, but

with the same breathlessness and shame. The same feelings of dread. They'd said everything they'd needed to say to each other, so why had he come all this way?

Crossing the street, she approached her house under Cash's direct gaze. She walked toward him as he advanced, and they met in the driveway. Near his car.

"I didn't know you were a runner." He smiled.

"Not as often as I should. What I really like is Pilates. I go to a class a couple times a week." Monica knew she was rambling, but really, why was he here? She stood toe to toe with him, her hands clenched at her sides. "What are you doing here?"

He ran a hand over his beard. "I'd like to go to your doctor's appointment with you. If you'll have me."

Monica chewed on that a minute. It didn't make any sense considering the way they'd left things between them. Besides, she was nervous enough without him tagging along. She wasn't sure she wanted him there to hear all the gruesome details. "I don't know…"

Cash gestured toward the house. "Can we go inside and talk about this?"

That sounded lengthy and even more alarming. She managed a smirk. "Are you nuts, on a nice day like this?"

"Humor me."

Monica didn't know where the urge to argue with him came from, but she dug in her heels. "What if I don't want to?"

His eyes darkened and a smile hovered at the corners of his shapely mouth. He stepped even closer. "I could carry you in."

Of course he could, but it still made her laugh; a nervous-sounding giggle escaped when she saw the look of determination in his eyes. He'd do it. She could just imagine him carrying her up those porch steps like some long floor rug draped over his shoulder.

She backed up, but his car was in the way.

Nothing stopped Cash. He slid his arms around her waist as if he'd scoop her up romantic-like, and whisk her up the steps and into her house as if…

She pushed against his chest. "Whoa…wait—"

He froze, looking serious. "Don't you think we've waited long enough and wasted enough time?"

She bit her lip. That was dangerous talk. Reckless even, considering their futures were so unsettled. Staring into his steady gray eyes, Monica decided she might need a little reckless. Especially now.

Throwing her arms around his neck, she answered Cash's question the best way she knew how. By covering his lips with her own.

With a contented chuckle, he gave in and kissed her back. There was nothing tentative or forlorn or even regretful about this kiss. With the determination and grit of a marine on a mission, Cash kissed her thoroughly.

She had a feeling he wouldn't apologize for this one, and she wouldn't, either. Her knees gave out, but he held her upright by pressing her against his car, never breaking away.

He kissed her with abandon. Right there in the driveway.

In the distance she heard a horn, followed by someone giving them a catcall whistle.

Monica came to her senses and broke for air.

He still had her pinned against the driver's side and his eyes glittered dangerously, sending a shiver through her. "I love you, Monica. That's why I'm here. Now, let's go inside."

Her mouth opened, but nothing came out. The swirling sensation of his declaration made her dizzy with joy. He loved her! Like a dunce, she didn't respond. She merely nodded and let him lead her by the hand through her front door.

Chapter Fourteen

Cash gave Monica an aggravated look when her front door opened at his touch. "Don't you keep it locked?"

"Not always. This is Maple Springs, you know." She sounded saucy, but gripped his hand as if holding on for dear life, or maybe balance.

He'd kissed her like a wild man, and he loved her befuddled expression because of it. He stepped inside the small bungalow that was Monica's house. The warm light oak floors were barely covered by colored area rugs that led to two pink floral couches perpendicular to a large brick fireplace painted white. Looking around, he noted that she had a deft hand at decorating. Her place resembled something from one of those renovation shows he'd seen on TV.

They walked into a decidedly white kitchen with red accents before she finally let go of his hand. "Cash—"

He touched his index finger to her lips, cutting her off again. He had to get this out before she brought up objections she was bound to throw his way. "Monica, I'm leaving Saturday, but I want to go to this appointment with you. You need to know that I've got your back."

Her beautiful brow furrowed. "I don't want the military life and I definitely don't want you worried about me when you're deployed."

Cash spread his arms wide and grinned. "Too late, baby. Even if you hadn't told me about the cancer, after this weekend, I'd never get you out of my head. I want more than what we were. A lot more. I've been thinking about making some changes. Maybe it's time to pull back behind the lines until I can retire."

Her eyes filled with hope, then darkened with challenge. "I have an aggressive form of breast cancer. I might need a mastectomy."

She'd never been one to mince words. That information sliced through him worse than the knife wound that had left him scarred across the gut. He could tell her that it didn't matter, but that would be a lie. He hated the idea of her going under the knife, but whatever it took to keep her with him, he was all in.

He wanted her to understand that whatever she needed, it wouldn't change how he'd love her. He tipped his head. "You see, I've always been a leg man—"

She punched his arm. "I'm serious."

"I'm serious, too." He sobered and quit teasing. "I'd rather you have surgery and live a long healthy life. One that includes me."

Her eyes widened, but she remained silent.

He could tell she doubted his words, maybe even his sincerity. In hindsight, teasing her hadn't been wise, so he went back in with big guns. "During this next deployment, if I lose a limb, will you feel differently about me? Will you walk away because of it?"

"No." Her voice was firm and full of conviction but

she still closed her eyes and clenched her fists as if trying to get control.

He cupped her chin, making her look at him. He didn't like the dark circles under her eyes that spoke of restless nights. "I'm not walking away, either. No matter what."

She stared at him for what felt like an eternity.

After that kiss, he had a clue as to what her feelings might be, but he could use some verbal encouragement about now, some kind of wave forward. He'd keep up a strong frontal assault until her defenses weakened. "I want to go with you to your doctor's appointment."

"I heard you the first time!" She actually snarled at him.

He yanked on her ponytail. "Then answer me already."

"You're crazy, you know that?"

He'd heard the catch in her voice and knew he'd weakened her resolve to keep him out of this. "Why? Because I finally admitted that I love you? What's crazy is that it took me this long to man up and say something. Crazier still is that I let you leave that cabin without telling you, accepting that we had no future because of what-ifs. Neither of our futures is set, so what kind of rationale was that?"

Monica looked skeptical, so he kept going. "I want to be with you every step of the way. Video calls, texts, phone calls, you name it. Whatever it takes, Stork, I'm not leaving you to face this battle without me, and just so you know, I'm pretty good in a fight."

Tears welled in her eyes. "But what if it's not enough and the cancer comes back?"

That possibility seared hot and sharp. Thinking about how his sister-in-law had never once regretted her time with Cole, Cash experienced what she meant, deep down and with unwavering resolve. "After all the time we wasted, don't you think we're worth a shot at forever, for however long or short that might be?"

She sniffed, but tears dripped off her golden lashes and rolled down her cheek. "I'm scared."

He brushed one away with his thumb, then slipped his arms loosely around her trim waist. "God knows we're both scared, but He's got this thing covered. He's got *us* covered. The Lord stole death's sting, remember? Since you left the cabin, I've been praying and digging in the Bible for something, anything that might bring me some peace, and it hit me. I finally realized that it's not up to me to beat death. It's up to me to trust in the One Who holds those keys."

She finally smiled then. Really smiled. Her face shone with a brilliance he hadn't seen all weekend. "I've loved you since I was twelve years old."

He laughed and pulled her forehead down to rest against his. "Remember when you wanted to make the varsity basketball team?"

"You helped me with my foul shot."

"Because you badgered me to. You never let me leave your house until I'd shot baskets with you. You never quit, Monica. Not once. And you made the team." He brushed a strand of hair off her face along with another tear. "This will be the fight of your life, but you're going to make the survivors team. We both are."

He heard her take a deep breath. "My mom's picking me up in less than two hours. Do you mind if she drives?"

"Not at all." He could hold her then, comfort her if needed.

She pulled away from him. "I better go shower."

He chuckled and waved at his nose, teasing her again. "Yeah, you should."

Her cheeks turned red, but she grinned. "Have you had lunch yet?"

"No, but I'll make something while you're getting ready."

She grabbed a towel from the hall closet, then turned and blew him a flirty kiss. "Make me some, too."

"Sure thing." Cash laughed it off, but the look she gave him was like no adrenaline rush he'd ever experienced.

Life with Monica promised to be one exciting thrill ride. One that would last their whole lives together.

Later that evening Cash opened his car door for her, but Monica didn't get in. "Can't we cancel? I'd rather not go."

Cash gave her a coaxing smile. "No, we're not going to cancel. Your mom wants us to come for dinner. Your brothers and sisters will be there. Most of them, anyway."

She dropped her head back and gazed at the sky. "That's why I don't want to go. Everybody's going to want to know how it went today and—"

He kissed the end of her nose. "Because they love you and they're rallying around you. Besides, this way you only have to say it all once."

"You've got a point." She knew he was right, and if she didn't go, she'd have a slew of phone calls to deal with, especially from her two sisters.

With a sigh, she slipped into the passenger seat.

He buckled her in and kissed her quickly.

She rolled her eyes at his fussing. "I'm not fragile."

"No. You're a warrior and I've never been more proud of you."

She swallowed hard and managed a rough sounding, "Thank you. I'm glad you were with me."

"Me, too." He caressed her cheek before shutting her door.

She watched as he circled the front of the car and tapped on the hood before climbing in the driver's side. He buckled in, hit the ignition button and revved the engine. Having Cash by her side today had indeed given her courage. He'd heard what she'd heard—the answers to her many questions.

Although much depended on how she responded to chemo, Monica had decided on an aggressive approach. She'd start chemotherapy right away to hopefully shrink the tumor and kill the cancer cells. Even if the tumor diminished in size, she was still going for a mastectomy. She wanted to stop the disease in its tracks, since it hadn't yet touched her lymph nodes. Removing all the tissue instead of just until a clean margin was reached seemed more reasonable in lessening the chances of cancer returning.

But it was still scary.

Cash drove the ten miles to her parents' place in record time. He drove fast on the long stretch of back road, but she didn't complain or bother to tell him to slow down. It was daylight, making it easy to scour the roadsides and fields for any deer. Besides, it was fun flying over the dips and valleys in his Dodge, reminiscent of the hilly trail they'd taken with the side-by-sides.

Midway there, Cash held her hand.

She didn't let go.

When they pulled up at her parents' home they had to squeeze in between her siblings' cars, which lined the driveway. It appeared they were the last ones to arrive. Squaring her shoulders, Monica got out and waited for Cash.

He came around and offered his hand again.

She took it, squeezing tightly as they ambled up the slate walkway to the front porch.

At the door, Cash stalled her. "I'm going to talk with your dad."

"Cash…" She didn't want to think about marriage until after her surgery. Not until she knew the cancer was gone.

He waved her objection away. "I just want to give him a heads-up and I'd rather do it in person. Nothing official."

"I wish you'd wait." She let go of his hand, opened the door and braced for impact.

Cash had always fit well into her family, but as a friend of her brothers. Tonight, it'd be pretty clear that he was her *boyfriend*.

"Hey, Cash!" Her brother Cam slapped him on the back. "What's this I hear about you and Monica?"

"I finally got up the courage to ask her out." Cash gave her a wink.

"I thought you were up at Uncle John's cabin with your nephews, so when was the date?"

"Today, at the doctor's office." Cash gave him an insolent smirk.

"Memorable, I'm sure." Cam nodded with approval, but he looked concerned.

Her whole family had those stress lines around their mouths, as if trying to show a strong front for her sake.

Maybe her mom had given them all a heads-up. Maybe Monica wouldn't have to rehash everything.

"'Bout time you asked her out. Come in and watch the game." Her brother Darren shook Cash's hand, then led him into the living room for a Lions preseason football game against the Cleveland Browns.

Monica watched him go, feeling like part of her was missing, though Cash had only gone into the next room. How was she going to stand it with him gone for months when she could barely let go of him now? Months on assignment where the possibility of him losing a limb or worse was all too real to think about. She would, though. Constantly.

Trust in the One who holds those keys.

That's what Cash had told her. It was the realization he'd come to after digging into scripture. After all his losses, she owed it to him. Owed it to herself to do the same. It was time to really trust God. Placing her life and Cash's in His hands regardless of the outcome was what faith was all about, wasn't it?

Her sister Cat elbowed her in the side, drawing her attention. "Mom said he was a rock at your doctor's appointment."

Cat held her eleven-month-old daughter against her hip, so Monica reached out her hands for the baby. Opal giggled, going right into her arms.

Monica bounced her a couple times before answering her sister. "Yeah."

"So, what's going on with you two?"

"We're together now." Monica let that statement sink in and simmer.

Cat smiled. "That's good. I think he always had his eye on you."

That was news to Monica. Had she been the only one who didn't understand why he'd somewhat avoided her, especially as she'd gotten older?

"How was it? The appointment."

"Uphill battle ahead. I start chemo next week."

Her sister's eyes widened. Evidently their mom hadn't clued everyone in. She'd left that up to Monica.

"Whatever it takes, we'll get through this. I'm right in town, not far from you. We'll do this," Cat said.

"Thanks." Monica had been wrong to think she'd face this disease alone.

How different things were now than when she'd first arrived at her uncle's cabin. She not only had family support and Cash, but her oncology team had given her the link to an online support group for triple negative breast cancer patients, as well. She could get more information from women who were going through or had gone through what she faced. When it came time for surgery, she'd rally her troops and march forward.

Cash would most likely be gone for most of it, either in training exercises or deployed, but she knew he'd be with her in thoughts and prayer. She'd be with him the same way. She'd trust that God would see them both through whatever happened.

In the past, she'd always feared the worst for Cash and that had kept her from really loving him. Now, she'd love him with the hope that he'd return to her. That he'd make it back alive, that some other position might become available to him until he could eventually retire from the marines in five years.

That was a long way off yet. She didn't want to daydream too far out. She'd focus on today, and tomorrow and then next week.

She wandered into the family room, where most everyone was watching the game while her mom and her brother Cam finished dinner preparations. Over the baby's head Monica caught Cash's gaze and held it.

He gave her a soft smile.

She returned it. Was he perhaps thinking about that game they'd played at the cabin, when she'd asked him for a pink peg? Would they have a baby girl or boy of their own one day? All unanswerable questions.

She wrestled back her thoughts. She was getting way ahead of herself, nearly as bad as Cash wanting to clear a marriage proposal with her father before she'd even allow him to ask her. One step at a time; she'd meant that.

Cash got up and walked toward her. "Who's this?"

"My niece, Opal." Monica tipped her head as the toddler grabbed a handful of her hair and yanked.

Cash loosened the locks from Opal's grip and smoothed them against her shoulder. "You look good with her."

Monica scrunched her nose to get rid of the catch in her throat. She wanted kids and prayed she'd have them one day. With Cash.

God answers prayer.

"Yeah?"

"Yeah." He looked like he wanted to say something else, but stroked her hair instead and gave her shoulder a comforting squeeze as if reading her thoughts. "I'm going to get water. Want a glass?"

She shook her head. "Maybe later."

He headed for the kitchen.

Monica stepped toward the family room and noticed her brothers and sisters staring at her. "What?"

"Nothing." Her siblings responded together as if in a chorus. Then they played innocent, looking away as if they hadn't just watched the brief exchange between her and Cash.

Sitting on the love seat, Monica let her squirming niece down and laughed when Opal ran, giggling the whole way, to Cat's waiting arms. Looking up, Monica spotted Cash talking to her father.

Her stomach flipped.

So much for one step at time. He ought to know better than to make plans to win the war before fighting the next battle. She needed to focus first on getting well, and trust that God would align the rest of their lives. She'd have faith in His perfect timing over her own.

Seven months later, Monica adjusted the scarf covering her still rather bare head and picked up her tablet, clicked into video conferencing and waited for Cash to call, as he'd texted he would.

Suddenly, his clean-shaven face took up the whole screen. "Hey, Stork."

"Hi."

"How are you feeling?"

"Pretty good, actually." She truly meant it this time.

She'd never wanted Cash worried or distracted by her health, and had refused to let him see her down or sick. When she had looked horrible because of broken capillaries in her face from throwing up after chemo, she'd texted him that she was tired and going to bed early for a whole week. She hoped God didn't fault her for lying so many times, but she did it to protect the man she loved.

That man backed up and she saw him fully and laughed.

Cash Miller had shaved his head and he wore a pink bandanna around his neck. "The guys have something they want to ask you."

Spanning back farther, the camera picked up a group of his men, standing amid the dusty terrain of who knew where they were. As one, they took off their hats. They, too, were all bald and each one wore a pink bandanna.

Tears gathered in her eyes at the sight of such support for her and the respect these men had for their first sergeant. Then they held up cardboard squares and her breath caught when the first guy flipped his around.

It read: *Monica.*

She had an idea what this was all about, but who did this kind of thing anymore? Cash Miller, that's who.

The next guy flipped his: *Will.*

Then the next: *You.*

PLEASE.

Marry.

Cash.

Miller?

Tears ran freely down her face by the time Cash was back in focus. He'd asked her this before and she'd stalled him every time. She had wanted to wait until after chemo and surgery. All that was over now, along with the nausea. Pain she'd handled pretty well with meds, and even those she hadn't needed to finish. She'd switched to plain old ibuprofen.

She'd been very blessed that the tumor had responded so well to the chemo that she could have opted for a lumpectomy. She still chose to go through with a single mastectomy and was able to have reconstruction in conjunction with a total skin-saving surgery.

Cash had supported her decision without hesitation. He said that he didn't care about reconstruction, but she did. Big time.

At her last doctor's appointment, she'd been given a promising outlook. She was finally on the mend and healing up nicely. Another two months or so and Cash would be able to take a short leave when his unit returned to the States.

"So, what's it going to be, Stork?" Cash waited.

"So, it's going to be a big fat yes." Monica breathed deep.

"When?"

She laughed, but really, he should know the answer to that. She braved up and took off the scarf to show him what she described as peach fuzz covering her head. "When I have hair."

He narrowed his gaze, but the smile never left his face. "How much hair?"

There's no way she'd be a bride with a buzz cut, so it was going to be a while yet. "Enough to look nice in pictures."

Cash turned serious. "That's now, baby, because you look beautiful."

Her throat tightened and her eyes watered some more. He had a way of making her *feel* beautiful, and she loved him all the more for it. Running her finger over the screen, she outlined his dear face, missing him terribly. "Thanks, Cash. You do the bald thing pretty well, too."

He smiled. "We'll figure it all out next time I'm home."

She gave him a salute. "Yes, sir."

"That's yes, First Sergeant, sir. Gotta go." He kissed his fingers and placed them on the screen. "I love you."

She did the same. "I love you more. See ya."

"Later." With a wink from eyes that also looked a little watery, he was gone.

Monica disconnected. They were apart, sure, but they would never again say goodbye—not in texts or emails, and they never would.

Taking a deep breath, she grabbed the sparkly note-book and matching pen Ruth Miller had given her. Cash's sister-in-law had visited her a couple times and they'd become fast friends. She brought the boys, after Monica had encouraged her to. Owen had been precious, holding her hand and telling her she was still pretty. Ethan had drawn her a picture of the four of them at her uncle's cabin with sparklers.

A thought suddenly hit her, so she wrote it down. Remembering her mother's wise advice to have fun while she was at her uncle's cabin, she knew exactly what she was after. She got busy making a list, because she had a big wedding to plan and it was going to be fun.

Epilogue

Cash stood at the altar and waited while seemingly hundreds of candles were being lit around him and up the aisle, where Monica would soon meet him. He wasn't nervous, but standing still was a challenge.

"Easy, big fella." Monica's brother Matthew stood next to him as his best man.

"Where is she already?" he whispered back.

"I don't know. Maybe she wants to make a grand entrance by being a little late."

Cash checked his watch, to the amused murmur of the guests. They were over ten minutes behind schedule.

Scanning the crowd, he smiled at the large number. Monica's mom and family members took up several rows, while his family managed to fill only one pew. His mom sat in the front, along with Ruth and his nephews. The boys had trouble sitting still, too. His sister-in-law looked ready to take them both outside by their ears.

The early evening sun filtered through the stained glass, casting colored patterns on the floor. Some of the colors reminded him of how he'd felt about Monica at the cabin, when he'd wielded those brilliant-hued crayons. That had been over a year ago, and so much had happened since then.

Checking his watch once again, he hoped they'd get outside in time. Monica wanted their wedding pictures taken at sunset by Maple Bay. They'd been blessed with a beautiful mid-October day. Mild temperatures and sunny.

If she ever got here.

The light classical music pumping over the sound system stopped and the live organist began playing some other kind of classical piece. That was a good sign they were ready to begin.

The back doors of the church opened and Monica's sister Cat walked toward him, smiling until she took her place at the altar. Another good sign.

Cash rubbed his damp palms against his trousers. This was it. Today was the day he'd become a husband. Today he'd tell his *wife* that he'd accepted a new role within the Marine Raider Regiment. The organ music changed to the traditional bridal march and everyone stood.

He took one look at Monica and swore his heart stopped for at least a second or two before pounding so hard his ears rang.

She was stunning in a lace halter dress the color of candlelight that shimmered as she walked down the aisle on the arm of her father.

Her hair had grown back wavy and it was a little darker than before. The golden-honey tone suited her, as did the short cap of curls that showed off the length of her graceful neck. She didn't wear a veil, but a headband with a spray of sparkly stuff to one side.

The closer she came toward him, the better he could see her bright blue eyes and the happiness he read there.

It matched his own, so he grinned at her.

She smiled back.

The beginning of the ceremony whizzed by in a blur until her father offered him Monica's hand. Taking it, he leaned close to her and whispered, "What took you so long?"

"I misplaced my 'something old' pin." She tipped her bouquet of a handful of lilies wrapped with ribbon. On the ribbon was a sparkly stork pin.

He shrugged, not understanding the "old" reference, but loving the pin. She'd always be his *Stork*.

"Something old, something new, something borrowed, something blue," she hissed.

He figured her dress was new. She'd confirmed that the stork pin was old. He didn't care what she'd borrowed, but was curious about what might be blue. He couldn't see that color anywhere. "What's blue?"

She gave him a pointed look as the clergyman cleared this throat. "Pay attention."

Another murmur of laughter emanated from the guests.

Cash grinned again. He'd ask later.

He looked forward to showing Monica the acceptance letter for his new position, which rested in the coat pocket of the dress blues he was wearing. After sixteen years of active duty, it was time to work behind the lines for a while. At least for the next four years, until he could retire and they could perhaps raise a family.

They had a lot of living to do now that they'd postponed death. They both wore battle scars that reminded them how close they'd come to it. Time seemed more precious now. Time together, priceless. He prayed that from here on out they wouldn't venture anywhere near death's door until the Lord called them home in their old age.

"Do you, Cassius William Miller, take Monica Marie Zelinsky to be your wedded wife?"

Cash looked into Monica's eyes and got lost there. "Yes, I do."

Monica waited for the master of ceremonies to announce their names before entering the reception hall at the Maple Springs Inn. They'd just returned from the beachfront, where they'd taken photos against a gorgeous sky at sunset. It couldn't have been more perfect. Like everything in her life right now.

It had been fourteen months since she was diagnosed with triple negative breast cancer. At her one-year follow-up there had been no sign of cancer, and Monica couldn't have been more grateful. Or blessed. God's timing was perfect.

Hearing their guests cheer was their cue to enter.

"Wait till you see this." Monica hooked her arm through Cash's. "I got the idea from your nephews."

She'd planned their wedding down to the finest detail and it had been remarkable therapy while she'd recovered. It had also been a fun diversion from selling her house and moving back home with her parents while she waited for Cash's extended leave for their wedding.

"What'd you do?"

"Come see." She pulled Cash forward into the large space, which had a dance floor set up in the middle.

They marched past guests lined up waving sparklers. Owen and Ethan were front and center, waving and twirling their sparklers just like they had at the cabin.

Folks pointed toward the dance floor, where they would join Cat and Matthew, each dancing with their spouse to an upbeat love song. Monica had chosen this first number with care after listening to dozens of lyrics. Titled "You and Me," the song was of course romantic, but also perfect. The tempo was more lively, positive and carefree sounding, but the words resonated deeply. She'd loved the message that together, the two of them could do anything.

Monica believed that was indeed true, because after all these years, they were here. Together and working on their forever.

"Nice touch with those sparklers," Cash whispered in her ear as he pulled her into his arms. "Nice song, too. I guess it will be ours from now on."

"Yes, it will, but we will find more, I'm sure."

They'd never danced together before and Monica was surprised at how smooth his movements were. Cash led her with confidence around the dance floor, twirling her in and out of his arms. There were so many things she wanted them to do together, new things they'd never done before, starting with their honeymoon on Hilton Head Island.

At least they'd have a solid week together before he was called somewhere for a mission. Biting her bottom lip, she tucked her head against Cash's and held on a little tighter.

"What?" He knew her so well.

"Nothing. Just looking forward to spending time alone together after all this."

He chuckled and gave her a squeeze. "The party is just getting started."

"I know, but—"

"I was going to wait until later to tell you this, but now seems like the right time." Cash stopped dancing and pulled an official-looking piece of paper from inside his uniform.

The song ended and the MC invited others to join the wedding party as dance mix music pounded out around them.

Monica took the paper from his hands and read the news that Cash had been assigned to special operations training at the Marine Raider Training Center at Camp Lejeune.

Smiling, she looked up at him. "When did you do this?"

"I put in for it a while ago, before you finally agreed to marry me."

Monica wrapped her arms around him, enjoying the strength of his returned embrace. "Thank you."

"I love the marines, Stork, but I love you even more."

She laughed. "Today couldn't get any more perfect."

Cash rubbed his nose against hers.

Monica took a deep breath, nervous about later.

"It'll be okay." Cash kissed her quickly.

Remembering the angry-looking mark on Cash's stomach, she relaxed. She not only believed him, but she trusted him. They were both warriors with battle scars, and although they had fought different wars, God had brought them both out victorious.

Monica threaded her fingers through his and squeezed. "It will be better than okay."

Together, they'd become whole by placing their trust in the One Who stole the sting of death and held the keys of their life firmly in His hands.

* * * * *

*Pick up these other stories in
Jenna Mindel's Maple Springs Series:*

Falling for the Mom-to-Be
A Soldier's Valentine
A Temporary Courtship
An Unexpected Family
Holiday Baby

Available now from Love Inspired!

*Find more great reads at
www.LoveInspired.com*

Dear Reader,

I hate cancer for what it does and the wreckage it leaves behind. I, like many of you, have friends and family who have been touched by this awful disease. I was halfway into writing this book when my brother was diagnosed with a rare form of throat cancer and that really brought this subject much too close to home. As I write this, his treatments are complete and his outlook is very good. I thank God for His healing!

By choosing a heroine with cancer, I wanted to honor those who've been there before. Monica has never been comfortable in her own skin and that plays deep into her insecurities at the start of this book. What I love about her is that she becomes a true warrior who overcomes those insecurities supported by the unwavering love of the hero, as well as her trust in God.

Living a redeemed life doesn't mean we won't face trials or even end up with cancer. But we do have a God Who walks with us in this imperfect life whether our race is long or cut short.

My prayer is that we keep our eyes fixed on the eternal prize and live the life God gave us, focused on Him.

Jenna

I love to hear from readers. Please visit my website at www.jennamindel.com or follow me on www.Facebook.com/authorjennamindel or drop me a note c/o Love Inspired Books, 195 Broadway, 24th Floor, New York, NY 10007.

COMING NEXT MONTH FROM
Love Inspired®

Available August 19, 2019

SHELTER FROM THE STORM
North Country Amish • by Patricia Davids
Pregnant and unwed, Gemma Lapp's determined to return to her former home in Maine. After she misses her bus, the only way to get there is riding with her former crush, Jesse Crump. And when he learns her secret, he might just have a proposal that'll solve all her problems...

HER FORGOTTEN COWBOY
Cowboy Country • by Deb Kastner
After a car accident leaves Rebecca Hamilton with amnesia, the best way to recover her memory is by moving back to her ranch—with her estranged husband, whose unborn child she carries. As she rediscovers herself, can Rebecca and Tanner also reclaim their love and marriage?

THE BULL RIDER'S SECRET
Colorado Grooms • by Jill Lynn
Mackenzie Wilder isn't happy when her brother hires her ex-boyfriend, Jace Hawke, to help out on their family's guest ranch for the summer. Jace broke her heart when he left town without an explanation. But can he convince her he deserves a second chance?

REUNITED IN THE ROCKIES
Rocky Mountain Heroes • by Mindy Obenhaus
Stopping to help a pregnant stranded driver, police officer Jude Stephens comes face-to-face with the last person he expected—the woman he once loved. Now with both of them working on a local hotel's renovations, can Jude and Kayla Bradshaw overcome their past to build a future together?

A MOTHER FOR HIS TWINS
by Jill Weatherholt
First-grade teacher Joy Kelliher has two new students—twin little boys who belong to her high school sweetheart. And if teaching Nick Capello's sons wasn't enough, the widower's also her neighbor...and competing for the principal job she wants. Will little matchmakers bring about a reunion Joy never anticipated?

HOMETOWN HEALING
by Jennifer Slattery
Returning home with a baby in tow, Paige Cordell's determined her stay is only temporary. But to earn enough money to leave, she needs a job—and her only option is working at her first love's dinner theater. Now can Jed Gilbertson convince her to stay for good?

LOOK FOR THESE AND OTHER LOVE INSPIRED BOOKS WHEREVER BOOKS ARE SOLD, INCLUDING MOST BOOKSTORES, SUPERMARKETS, DISCOUNT STORES AND DRUGSTORES.

LICNM0819

SPECIAL EXCERPT FROM

*On her way home, pregnant and alone,
an Amish woman finds herself stranded
with the last person she wanted to see.*

Read on for a sneak preview of
Shelter from the Storm *by Patricia Davids,
available September 2019 from Love Inspired.*

"There won't be another bus going that way until the day after tomorrow."

"Are you sure?" Gemma Lapp stared at the agent behind the counter in stunned disbelief.

"Of course I'm sure. I work for the bus company."

She clasped her hands together tightly, praying the tears that pricked the backs of her eyes wouldn't start flowing. She couldn't afford a motel room for two nights.

She wheeled her suitcase over to the bench. Sitting down with a sigh, she moved her suitcase in front of her so she could prop up her swollen feet. After two solid days on a bus she was ready to lie down. Anywhere.

She bit her lower lip to stop it from quivering. She could place a call to the phone shack her parents shared with their Amish neighbors to let them know she was returning and ask her father to send a car for her, but she would have to leave a message.

Any message she left would be overheard. If she gave the real reason, even Jesse Crump would know before she reached home. She couldn't bear that, although she

LIEXP0819

didn't understand why his opinion mattered so much. His stoic face wouldn't reveal his thoughts, but he was sure to gloat when he learned he'd been right about her reckless ways. He had said she was looking for trouble and that she would find it sooner or later. Well, she had found it all right.

No, she wouldn't call. What she had to say was better said face-to-face. She was cowardly enough to delay as long as possible.

She didn't know how she was going to find the courage to tell her mother and father that she was six months pregnant, and Robert Troyer, the man who'd promised to marry her, was long gone.

Don't miss
Shelter from the Storm *by* USA TODAY
bestselling author Patricia Davids,
available September 2019 wherever
Love Inspired® books and ebooks are sold.

www.LoveInspired.com

Copyright © 2019 by Patricia MacDonald

LIEXP0819